To my dear friends,
Geri and Lou,
May your life be like
a great round of golf — all
pars and birdies!
Happy Reading!

Love,
Arlene

STRAND PRICE
5.00

PUTTING FOR THE GREEN

by
Margaret Flynn and Arlene Scollar

authorHOUSE®

AuthorHouse™
1663 Liberty Drive, Suite 200
Bloomington, IN 47403
www.authorhouse.com
Phone: 1-800-839-8640

© 2008 Margaret Flynn and Arlene Scollar. All rights reserved.

No part of this book may be reproduced, stored in a retrieval system, or transmitted by any means without the written permission of the author.

First published by AuthorHouse 12/12/2008

ISBN: 978-1-4389-0753-6 (sc)
ISBN: 978-1-4389-0752-9 (hc)

Printed in the United States of America
Bloomington, Indiana

This book is printed on acid-free paper.

To my husband, Dermot, my daughter, Beth, and grandaughter, Lucy May, who provide my base in reality and encourage my creativity.

MARGARET MANNIX FLYNN

To my dearest husband, Sam, wonderful children, Allison and Adrienne, and the fabulous four, Olivia, Abigail, Jack and Addison.

ARLENE ALTON SCOLLAR

High Ridge Country Club Locker Room, Westchester, New York, May 2nd

The second martini was beginning to do its job. Peter flexed his legs and leaned back on the teak bench, resting his head on the marble wall of the sauna. The tension was leaving his body, and the desperation he felt was washing away. Hopefully the loan sharks could be appeased with the money he would win playing in the Country Club Golf Tournament.

He took another sip of his martini and set his glass beside him on the bench. He began to doze, thinking of Valerie, his mistress, modeling the new French lingerie he had in the trunk of his Rolls. She was a caring woman, not like his wife. Valerie answered his every need in every way. Her skin was soft, and her lips were warm and welcoming.

"I don't give a flying fuck how good a player Peter Drummond is-- he is not going to represent the team in this tournament."

The voice was that of Henry (Hank) Hawthorne, Club President and top golfer at the club.

Peter jumped, upsetting the glass onto his towel. The voice was coming from the adjoining locker room through the vent over his head. "Aw, Hank, why are you so down on him," responded Bradford Wellington IV, a genial club member. Brad was a teddy bear of a man and saw good in everyone.

"Shit, Brad, the guy's a fucking cheat. You saw him 'adjust' his score when he missed his first chip shot on the eighth hole."

"Hank, I'm the first to abhor cheating, but Peter was not himself. He's been terribly distracted," Brad countered.

"It's a gentleman's game and Peter is no gentleman, he's a cheat. I am going to see that he will not represent us at the tournament."

Peter could not breathe. He felt ice cold sitting in the 120 degree sauna. He must be on that golf team. When that team wins, he will have the $200,000.00 that he desperately needs.

"Come on, Hank, we have to move along. Mildred said I have to be home by 5:00 p.m. for the cocktail bash she's giving. It's 4:50 now."

"Yeah, and I have to be at my stepdaughter's piano recital before 6:00. I hope she's learned to play. God knows I've paid enough for lessons."

Peter could hear the two of them depart through the squeaking locker room door. "Nothing will keep me off that team, and nothing will keep me from winning." Peter exited the sauna, leaving the martini glass on its side, dribbling out the remnants of Kettle One.

Horace Drummond, Peter's grandfather, made a large fortune in the 1900's, along with Carnegie and Mellon, in steel and railroads,. Peter's father, Lawrence, died while Peter was still in college. After establishing a trust for Peter's mother, the remainder of the assets was divided among the three sons, Frederick, Mark and Peter. The two older sons, who by now had established themselves as astute businessmen, each received one third of the estate outright. Peter, many years younger than his brothers had a life trust established for him. A stipend was drawn from this trust each year on Peter's birthday in September. The stipend was a sizable amount able to support Peter and his wife Gloria's lavish lifestyle. This included private schooling for their daughter, the family home next to the country club, and a 6,000 square foot home in Palm Springs. Peter did not own the two homes; they were part of his inheritance. He could use them, but not sell them.

Peter chafed with resentment that the trust did not allow access to his own inheritance. Consequently, he played the stock market to prove his ability in business. Peter was not a winner in the business world.

Now Peter was in trouble, his stock trading leaving him greatly in debt. Large bills were facing him: his daughter's tuition, his new Rolls Royce, his wife's cosmetic surgery and his mistress. He had no cash and no way to pay his expenses. He could no longer get a bank loan because his stipend required that he remain debt free. Otherwise, the yearly allowance would end.

Through a few visits to establishments of a dubious nature, he located shady people who lent money at an exorbitant rate.

That was three months ago. Last night as Peter was exiting his car a rough-voiced man accosted him. He held in his hand a wooden baseball bat that he tapped on the Rolls Royce fender and then on the concrete driveway. Back and forth he tapped each a little harder. At last he stuck the bat directly on Peter's throat, forcing his chin up, growling, that $200,000 was due on his high percentage loan within the month.

Then the man violently swung the bat, smashing one headlight before disappearing into the bushes. Peter was left shaken and sweating. He had no where to turn. Feeling caged and desperate, he did not sleep that night. He tossed and turned, and the bedclothes tangled about him.

Towards dawn he drifted off to sleep and awoke with a start. The Country Club Golf Tournament offered $250,000.00 to each member of the winning team. He would be on that team and win the money.

High Ridge Country Club
Sunday, May 3rd

Connie Carson stood before the country club bulletin board, her size four figure sporting a Jamie Sadock golf outfit. "Qualification for the million dollar tri-county tournament will take place next Saturday and Sunday," she read silently. "There are only 20 slots for qualifying and the entrance fee of $12,500.00 must be turned into the pro shop by May 3rd."

"Hmm, I'm not on call next weekend," she mused. Her partner, Cliff, was on the call roster for cardiology rotation at the hospital. "I wonder what the men would do if I competed?"

Connie was actually one of the few women members of the High Ridge golf club. Having posted a $75,000.00 bond gave her the privilege of playing before noon on weekends. All other women, wives of club members and a few widows of members, were relegated to afternoon tee off times.

Connie, a five handicapper, had taken up the game early. Being dirt poor Connie had no thought to such a "rich man's" game, but her older brother, Jason, wanted a golfing companion.

He had encouraged her to sneak with him onto the public golf course near their home. The old starter took pity, and turned a blind eye whenever he saw the teenagers silently coming through the fence. For some reason the fence was never repaired, and more eager teenagers joined Jason's group.

It was an old course, in disrepair, and not worth the time or money for the city to return it to its once pristine nature. A few times a year it would get fertilized, and when the mowers did not break down, it was kept in somewhat decent shape.

Finally one day the starter rode by in his golf cart and stopped by the thirteenth green where the teens were putting. "Hey, kids, one of the pro shop assistants has quit. One of you want the job? It means working after school, weekends and holidays. The plus side is you can legally play golf and also use the driving range when business is slow."

Jason and Connie looked at each other. Connie squeezed the putter so tightly her fingers turned white. She wanted that job, but it was Jason's right to take it first. "Thanks for for the offer, but football starts in a couple weeks, and I won't have time. What about you, Connie?"

Connie thanked God that Jason was the number one tight end on the local high school team. "I'll take it," she said with a smile. From that time on, Connie had a new life. She learned to be assertive when the regulars would try to bully her for a free round. She bought golf clothes off the ten dollar rack, and hit practice balls until dark when the other assistant was covering the shop.

Connie hated to go home at night--both her parents drank heavily and usually ended up pushing each other around. If it had not been for the high school mentoring program she probably would have dropped out at fifteen and run away. This program was run by the local Chamber of Commerce and paired high school students with business leaders.

Her junior year she tried out for the boy's golf team and made the number four position. She continued to work at the course, but her golf coach said it was the team or her job. She was missing too many practices and would be cut from the team.

Her mentor, Dr. Ben Johnson, an Internist, was apprised of the situation by the coach. Dr. Johnson knew that Connie wanted to become a doctor. Her one chance at this was a college scholarship. What better scholarship than a golf one? It didn't hurt that her high school had won the state championship. Plus, any girl who could decently hold a club was courted by colleges. Federal Title Nine gave equal opportunities for young women to compete on college sports teams. Colleges started vying for top women athletes.

All in all, a golf scholarship could be a shoo-in for Connie if she stayed on the team. Connie hadn't seen her mentor for awhile so was slightly apprehensive when she walked into his office.

"Grades still good, Constance?" The doctor always insisted calling her by her given name as if to give her a little stature. He knew her home situation merited some confidence-boosting from time to time.

"Great, doctor," replied Connie. " I take the SAT's next week."

Connie had a photographic memory and an analytical mind to go with it. "If you took her out of her home environment she could fit in with the finest families," mused the doctor. "Especially my family." She even looked like his wife, Emily, with her long chestnut hair and perky upturned nose. His wife and he had not been blessed with children, and thus he joined the mentoring program. Now he was a widower with more time on his hands. His wife had just passed away last year.

"I have a proposition for you. See if this meets your needs for college. Several anonymous donors wish to give you a monthly stipend to supplement any golf scholarship you might receive. No questions asked by you and no repayment. I would advise you to accept this offer."

"But, why, doctor? Why do this for me?"

"Because so many children your age just waste their lives on drivel. You are an excellent student with a 4.0 average. How could we find anyone more deserving than you?"

"I can't believe I'm being offered this opportunity. Since I need this so badly, I accept. I'll do my best to make you proud of me. Who are the other people helping me?" Connie wondered if possibly the doctor was making up the fact that there were others. She would not put it past him to just give her the money himself. She knew he felt she was like an adopted daughter.

"Sorry, Constance. Those are the provisions."

" Again, I accept, but medical school is mine. I won't accept any money after undergrad. Please honor my desire to make my own place in life."

College led to medical school (and big loans as Connie was true to her word), and now Connie was standing in the poshest club in New York. "I sure could use that money," Connie thought. " I have big outstanding med school loans, but I chose to put up that huge bond in order to further my medical career." Ruefully, she laughed to herself for the only recent referral generated by club membership was the golf pro's wife.

"So much for my affluent medical practice. I guess at 34 I still have plenty of time, but that money tournament could solve a lot of my problems. For $12,500 I could end up with a fortune."

Connie slipped into the pro shop and found the pro, Jimmy Lawson, re-gripping a member's club. "Hi, Jimmy, how is your wife doing? I have not seen her since her last appointment two months ago."

"Doc, that new blood pressure medication really did the trick. She takes her pressure every day, and it's been perfect. You're the only one who's been able to control it."

"You put too much faith in me, Jimmy, but I'm glad she's doing so well. Her other illness complicates matters, but I'm glad she's better. I thought for awhile we'd have to hospitalize her."

"That's all I'd need with a teenager in the home. Although Betsy never gives me a moment's worry. Do you know she had the smarts to walk out of a party where drugs were being used? I happened to hear her talking to a friend on the phone. I didn't mean to eavesdrop, but she didn't know I'd walked into the house."

Just then Chip Nelson and Hank Hawthorne came into the pro shop. Chip said, "Hey, Jimmy, I see you are finishing re-gripping my club. Just charge it to my account. By the way, when do you need my entrance fee for the money tournament? This million dollar tournament is a great idea."

"Don't forget," Jimmy said. "The club gets no cut. We don't want any legal problems. Your checks will be turned into cash and the money displayed at every participating team's club. Should make for excitement to have people see a million dollars. I guess a Brinks truck will have to follow it around!"

Connie pulled her checkbook out and quickly wrote her check, too. "Here's mine, Jimmy. I can't wait to tee up."

"Wait a minute," Hank said. "Are girls eligible?"

Connie gritted her teeth. "Good ol boy," Hank, was the height of the chauvinists. She often wished he'd go back to Alabama, but a company transfer to New York seemed permanent. With his southern charm he'd weaseled his way into the club presidency, but his philosophy was that men ruled, period.

"Hank, I don't see it written in the rules that WOMEN can't compete. I guess you're stuck with me. Maybe we'll be in the same group since you have a four handicap. Would you like me to tee the ball up for you each time? It must be hard to bend over with that belly." Turning her back to the men, she stalked out of the pro shop.

"Whoa," Hank sheepishly said. "No wonder she isn't married. That girl has a temper. Someone should pull down her panties and give her a good spanking. I might just be the one to do it."

"You seem to have brought out the beast in her," Chip noted sarcastically. "I thought southern men had women eating out of their hand. Her specialty is the heart, and I think she wanted to rip yours out."

Chip ran his fingers through his sandy blond hair and adjusted his glasses. Whenever he was nervous, the glasses came off. "Speaking of body damage, I'm out of here. My wife's family is coming over for a barbecue. Talk about pushing the wrong buttons--I need to be on my best behavior. Last time they came over I was an hour late. Bets had to be tallied--you'd think Babs would be happy to have an extra $500 to spend in Atlantic City. She goes there once a week." Chip took his club from Jimmy and walked out the door.

Hank turned around to Jimmy and noticed Jimmy's hand was shaking. "Maybe you need a little 'hair of the dog that bit you,' Jimmy. You hit the booze pretty good at the club last night. I thought I danced well with Mr. Jim Beam, but you were Fred Astaire."

Jimmy put his head in his hands. "Listen, Hank. We've been good friends since college days at Wake Forest. I'm telling you I've got to quit. It was all fine drinking my life away at the frat house, but I'm getting too old for this. Even Ann was mad at me last night, and she has the patience of a saint."

"She not only has the patience, she was the prettiest sweetheart of Sigma Chi. You were one lucky hound dog. I still remember singing on the Chi O front lawn when you pinned her. Too bad about the accident, Jimmy. You did right by marrying her."

"Right by marrying her! For Christ's sake, I put her in the wheelchair." Jimmy slapped his hand on the counter.

"Hey, Buddy, take it easy. What's done is done. Now to some serious club stuff. You can't let Carson compete next week. We'd be the laughingstock of all the clubs with a woman on the team. You've got to take care of it."

"Hank, what can I do--she has every right to try out."

"Jimmy, she's good enough to make it. You've got to stop her--get her disqualified."

"I can't do it."

"Let me remind you, Jimmy, your contract is up this year. There have been some rumblings about your drinking which I've squelched. Now you have to do this. You don't want to see the new young assistant pro take your place, do you?"

Jimmy knew what a popular pro, Ted Rankin, was. His appointment list for lessons was starting to overshadow Jimmy's. "God, Hank, I don't like that threat. I guess I'll see what I can do."

"Great, Jimmy. I think you'll find a new five-year contract on your desk next week. I've got the board members in my pocket. Also, I've just thought of a way to get Carson. You are always giving her lessons. Have her try a new driver and make certain it ends up in her bag. Fifteen clubs in her bag will get her penalties."

As Hank walked out Jimmy opened the drawer to his desk and pulled out a flask. Quickly he tipped it back, and let the smooth liquid run down his throat. Not too much, he thought as he put on the cap. Just enough to get me through this afternoon's lessons.

The Metrolpolitan Museum of Art
Wednesday Evening, May 6th

Babs Nelson stood before the Pyramid in the Egyptian Room of the Metropolitan Museum of Art. This was not her idea of a fun evening, but her friends made her attend. Babs would much prefer to be playing blackjack at Foxwood's or at AC.

This party was held yearly to raise money for Gloria Drummond's favorite charity so Valerie LaGrange, Millie Wellington, Sarah Hawthorne, Gloria and Babs were in New York City for the evening.

They were dressed for the occasion and Gloria's vintage Halston gown was in itself a work of art. Babs was happy to see Gloria enjoying herself. Gloria had returned from her cosmetic surgery in Costa Rica last week and this was her first big night out. She looked a little pale despite the fiery glow of her gown.

Sarah and Millie were approaching Babs waving their programs at her. Such a mismatched pair, Sarah lean elegance and Millie rounded relaxation. They were good friends, however. Millie worked hard to have Sarah feel welcome as the new wife in the group.

"Score one for our side," called Sarah. "The five of us are listed in the program as benefactors with no mention made of our husbands. Regardless of High Ridge Country Club's regulations we do exist as individuals without our husbands."

Millie giggled at this. She and Brad approached life as if joined at the hip. High school sweethearts and years of marriage had made them function as one, but she went along with Sarah's analysis.

Valerie LaGrange drifted towards them from the left and a news photographer appeared to be following her. "What's up?" asked Babs when they were within speaking distance.

"That photographer wants a picture of the five of us together," replied Valerie.

"Well, here comes Gloria, so it looks like he'll get his wish," said Babs. The five of them posed and their smiles and jewels were as dazzling as the flash from the camera.

"Well, here you are, at last I've found you all together." It was the voice of Collette Devereaux, columnist for the Westchester Weekly. "What are you lovelies doing out on the town without your husbands?" Collette demanded.

"The boys gave us the night off so they could plan their strategy for the upcoming golf tournament," replied Millie.

They're always playing golf. What's so different about this tournament?"

Millie looked at the others. Valerie shrugged in reply, so Millie went on. "The prize money for the winning team is one million dollars in cash."

Now, Collette was interested. She began to make mental notes as to when and where the tournament would be held and how the money would be collected and presented.

Gloria brought the conversation back to the purpose of the fund raiser and noted that all the guests were very cooperative in making contributions.

After a while, Collette and the photographer wandered off to the next group and the five women were alone. " I don't think it was such a good idea to tell Collette about the tournament," said Babs.

"Well, she'd find out sooner or later, so it's just as well that she heard it from us. At least from our telling, the facts will be accurate," replied Valerie.

"Always the editor," teased Babs, referring to Valerie's position at Premier Publishing.

The party was winding down and after attending to a few details, Gloria told her friends that she was tired and ready to leave. The others were somewhat surprised at this, but were happy to depart for Westchester.

Lake Mahopac
Wednesday, May 6th

"Come on, Laura, you know you want this. Come on, let yourself go." Chad Hawthorne goaded Laura as usual. He was starting back on the high school football team, handsome, arrogant, manipulative and Laura's steady boyfriend.

Laura Drummond held the marijuana cigarette in her hand and studied it. "I don't really need this, Chad. I do fine without it." Laura wrinkled her snub nose as she sniffed the weed. Her hazel eyes and auburn hair, a gift from her dad, Peter, shone in the setting sun.

Chad would not be put off. He got up from the grass, looked at the lake and without turning towards her said, "Laura, I'm your boyfriend. Get with the program. My friends think you're a wimp. You are the only one in our crowd who does not smoke pot. What's wrong with you?"

Laura could feel her chest tightening. She looked down at the grass she was sitting on and began to pull clumps of it out by the roots. She loved Chad, wasn't that enough? Why did she always have to prove herself to him. Couldn't he accept her as she is? It was no use. He would not let go. She gave up and lit the joint.

Silver Birch Spa
Thursday Morning, May 7th

The Silver Birch Spa is an exclusive retreat for the well-to-do. Nestled in the Berkshire Mountains, it is removed from the stresses of city living and dispenses comfort, pampering and relaxation. This was Gloria Drummond's favorite retreat. At the moment, she needed all that the spa had to offer. The tummy tuck and liposuction that she had done in Costa Rica two weeks ago left her feeling sore and exhausted.

It took all her strength and will to get through the fund raiser at the Metropolitan Museum of Art last night. She headed for the Silver Birch early the next day. The three hour drive exhausted her, and she spent most of Thursday dozing in her suite. Her dinner was delivered to her bedside on the finest china, but she ate very little.

Her thoughts drifted to Peter and Laura, but she decided she needed to take care of herself. Laura was already a senior and into her own friends. She had to look good for Peter, and their social circle. She fleetingly wondered what kind of a mother she was, but fell into a restless sleep before she could feel guilty.

Turner Academy
Thursday, May 7th

Chris LaGrange's bad luck started in his third period class when Mr. Herman called him aside and told him he was in danger of failing economics. Chris blurted out, "You can't fail me. I'm due to graduate in a few weeks. Failing this course will stop me from graduating."

Herman nodded and said, "That's your problem, Chris. You have seven homework assignments missing and you've failed three quizzes. Your project, which is fifty percent of your grade is due today and you don't have it."

"I'll catch up. I'll do extra work, you know I can pass this course."

"Yes, Chris, I know you can do better than pass, but you don't seem to want to do well. You have the ability, but not the desire. What's going on with you? You can be a good student."

"Things just got away from me. I got involved in a lot of things."

"Now's the time to get your priorities straight," responded Herman. The teacher did not want to fail Chris. He knew the boy could do the work. "I'll give you until Monday to bring in the project, but it has to show extra research and you have to relate your supply and demand topic to present day economic problems." Chris thanked him and promised to have the project in on Monday.

The day got worse. On the way home from school, he had an accident with his new Lexus. He was not paying attention and was driving too fast as he rounded a curve. The car fishtailed and the back hit a tree. The flexible rear bumper was pushed in on the passenger side and the paint was chipped off. Chris could still drive the car, but the dent could be seen at fifty feet. His dad had just given him the car for his eighteenth birthday. Damage to the car would cause his father to ground him or even take the car back. He was afraid of his father's anger.

Chris made his way to a body shop that did good work very quickly, but was also known for shady dealings. He pulled into the driveway. The owner, a tattooed man with a greasy ponytail, looked at the car and looked at Chris. "Your old man's car?"

"No," replied Chris. "Mine."

"That's a nice ride. You should take better care of it. That dent looks pretty sad. I suppose you want to get it fixed ASAP. Don't need your old man raggin' on you about it, now do you?"

"You got that right," replied Chris.

"With two hours work, I can pull out that dent from the bumper and fix the paint, but it'll cost you."

"How much?" demanded Chris.

"An expensive car calls for expensive work."

"What's your price?" asked Chris, losing his bravado.

"A rush job, but a good job. Let's say two thousand."

"Two thousand dollars?" gasped Chris in disbelief.

"Take it or leave it," smirked the owner. Just then the mechanic approached from the rear of the shop. He motioned the owner over to the back door.

"What's the action with the kid?" he demanded.

"He wants that bump fixed and painted ASAP. I gave him a big price. Right now, he's shittin' in his shoes."

"Maybe we can use him," the mechanic offered.

"How?"

"Well, he can't meet your price. So let's see if he can do us a favor instead." The mechanic's large gap teeth shone in a smile. "Let us see if he can help us develop some customers."

"He's yours. You do what you want. Just make sure that I get at least five hundred dollars for the job." With that the owner left by the back door.

The mechanic approached Chris who by now was breaking a sweat. "Hey, I got a proposition for you."

"What?" asked Chris hopefully.

"I'll fix your car for five hundred dollars and a favor."

"Sure," said Chris. He had almost six hundred in his savings account so he felt he was set.

"I understand that you want this job done good and done fast. I can make that happen for five hundred dollars and a favor."

"I'm ready."

"OK kid, this is the arrangement. I do the job for five hundred dollars and you spread some blow among your friends. Who knows, they might like it and come back for more. If you get my drift."

Chris was stunned. "My friends don't do heavy drugs, just a little weed now and then."

"Well this is your chance to be a man and step up to the big time." Gap Tooth smiled encouragingly.

Chris was now getting frightened. What was happening? This was dangerous stuff. "I'll think about it," he managed to whisper.

"Keep thinking and when you come to yes, then your car is fixed."

Chris groaned. He was afraid of his father and afraid of this man. "OK," he said at last. "I'll try to do what you ask ."

"Don't try. Do it or your car stays as it is."

"OK, OK, fix the car. I'll do it."

The car was ready as promised and while it was being repaired, Chris called Chad to take him to an ATM. Chad arrived, driving Laura's car. He immediately noticed that Chris was very nervous, but thought it was the result of the accident. He warned Chris to be fast as he had to return Laura's car in twenty minutes.

And that was it! Chris had his car back as good as new and he also had a small plastic bag of white powder. Gap Tooth assured Chris the cocaine had been cut with powdered milk so no one would OD.

Hawthorne Home
Thursday, May 7th

At the party were the usual Turner Academy High School football players and their dates. Chad's folks were away for the night and the kids had the run of the house, the pool and the wet bar.

By midnight everyone was thoroughly soaked--from chlorine water and beer. The pool area was littered with half- eaten sandwiches, flip flops and discarded clothing.

No one was fully dressed. Laura managed to be still wearing her bra and panties, but other girls were not.

Chris LaGrange stood on the diving board in his speedo holding a gym bag and called for attention. Slowly most of the group looked towards him.

"I have something for you. The highlight of the evening. Gather 'round and I will share it with you."

The kids moved to the picnic table set up behind the diving board. Chris had cleared away one end and placed a mirrored tray on the open space. Once the group had assembled he drew a stack of dollar bills from the bag and gave each of them one. Chris told them to roll the money into a straw shape.

Then he opened the gym bag and removed a small plastic bag of white powder from it. He began to pour narrow lines on the glass tray. The lines were side by side about three inches apart and three inches long.

"O.K. ladies and gentlemen," he said. "Start your engines."

That was the last thing Laura heard before the police sirens.

Long Hill Road
Thursday, May 7th

"Those damn kids and their boom boxes. We don't even get a peaceful school night with them." Jim Morrissey tossed his coffee cup out the car window and put the police cruiser into drive. Old Lady Watkins put in another noise complaint, the fifth in a two month period.

"Who says you get deaf as you age? The old lady is eighty- nine and can hear sand falling in an hour glass." The complaint stated that "abdominal noise" was coming from the Hawthorne home.

Morrissey flipped on the siren and headed up the twisting road to the Hawthorne residence. The Watkins' house was a good two hundred yards from Hawthorne's, so the old lady could see nothing, but apparently she could hear everything. Her list included: drumming disco, shrill shrieks and spasmodic splashing. Her background as an English teacher showed in her alliteration.

At the sound of the siren, Chad Hawthorne pulled on his clothes and headed for the front door of the mansion. The other kids tried as best they could to get dressed.

Chris LaGrange dumped the white powder into the pool chemicals stored behind the diving board and rinsed the mirror in the pool.

Charleen Dixon, co-captain of the cheerleaders, grabbed the mirror and began to dance with it on the diving board holding the mirror to shield her bare breasts and reflect the faces of the onlookers.

Laura pulled on her shirt and jeans and prayed that she would not throw up from fear. Morrissey was met by Chad on the front steps. "We got a call about a noise disturbance," he stated.

"That old woman has ears like a bat and no sense of how to have a good time. She should mind her own business," shouted Chad in response.

Morrissey realized that the Hawthornes were powerful people in town and he did not want any grief.

"Where are your folks?" he asked.

"My sister is at a friend's house and my parents are at the opera in New York City and won't be back until late."

How convenient for you, thought Morrissey "I have to investigate this complaint."

Chad did not put up a protest lest he draw attention to the presence of drugs. "Ok, follow me." He led the cop through the foyer, left into the dining room, past the kitchen and family room and out onto the pool deck moving as slowly as possible to allow the kids time to hide the beer bottles and remove evidence of drugs.

"Biff, turn off the music. Officer Morrissey is here," shouted Chad.

Biff Wellington turned an assortment of dials and the place fell silent. Thirty-two teenagers looked toward the French doors at the shallow end of the pool and faced Chad and Morrissey.

"All right," barked the cop. "What's going on here?"

Chris LaGrange was pulling on his black tee shirt over his wet body while trying to coax Charleen off the diving board. She giggled at his attempts. Flashing the mirror that she used to cover herself, she fell into the pool. The kids started to laugh.

Morrissey would have none of it. "Listen to me!" he boomed. "I'm here on a noise complaint, but I can see I can also add to it indecent exposure, underage drinking and who knows, perhaps even the use of illegal substances."

Every one fell silent, even Charleen, who was climbing out of the pool and reaching for a towel offered to her by Laura.

"Officer Morrissey," said Chad in a most placating manner. "This is the final party for the football team and their dates. Granted, we are a little loud, but no one lives closer than one hundred fifty yards to this house. We have a designated driver group anytime alcohol is used."

Morrissey recognized the lying he was listening to, but what could he do. The Hawthorne family were very influential and he was employed by the town. He felt he had to save face. "Ok, I'll tell you what," he snapped.

"The party ends now. You will all go home. The designated drivers will give me a list of who they are taking home. Cars can be left here to be picked up tomorrow. I will drive that young lady from the diving board home in the cruiser with one of her girl friends. I will now inspect the area around the pool while you all get ready to leave. No one departs until I say so. And remember tomorrow is Friday and it is a school day. I don't want any complaint that any of you are playing hooky."

This action on Morrissey's part was stronger than what was done when he broke up other teenage parties. When he got no complaint from them, he knew he was on to something. There were drugs here someplace. He prayed he would not find them. He valued his job.

After a preliminary walk around the pool deck, he nodded that he was satisfied and told the kids to leave as soon as he got the designated driver list. Laura Drummond volunteered to take the cruiser ride with Charleen. Chad said nothing to Laura when she left.

Lawson Home
Thursday, May 7th

Morrissey dropped a tired and hiccupping Charleen at her front door, where she was greeted by her not too happy parents. He then proceeded to take Laura to the Drummond home.

Laura spoke little during the trip. Her thoughts were on Chad and the mess that the party turned into.

Upon arrival at her home, Laura realized that she did not have a key. Ringing the bell brought no response. It was the help's night off, her mother was at a spa, recovering from last night's fund raiser and last week's cosmetic surgery, and her father evidently was not home. Morrissey insisted on driving her to stay at a friend's home. Laura asked him to take her to Betsy Lawson's. Betsy was at the party, but left when the marijuana was brought out.

A sleepy-eyed Betsy opened the door and was shocked to find Laura there with a policeman. "What happened? Are you all right?" she gasped.

"I'm fine." said Laura. "The party got out of hand and the police were called. Officer Morrissey made us all go home, but I could not go home because there was no one there to let me in." At this point the events of the evening caught up with her and she began to cry.

Officer Morrissey looked embarrassed and Betsy hugged Laura and soothed her as best she could.

"Are your parent's home?" asked Morrissey.

"Yes," said Betsy. "But they're asleep."

"Can this girl stay here tonight?"

"Of course, Laura and I are good friends. We often stay overnight at each other's homes. I'll leave a message on her dad's answering machine so he'll know where she is when he gets home."

"Thanks," said Morrissey and left.

Betsy was happy to see him leave. Her dad was drinking more heavily than usual. He seemed to be worried about his job at the pro shop. Betsy did not want Morrissey to see Jimmy Lawson stumbling around the house.

After Betsy got an exhausted Laura into bed, she left a message on the Drummond phone. She knew Mrs. Drummond was at a spa, but where was Mr. Drummond? How inconsiderate not to care about Laura.

Finally Betsy tried to get some sleep herself, but it was not easy. She worried about Chad's influence on Laura. He had a very strong personality, and Laura liked to please him.

The Plaza Hotel
Friday Early Morning, May 8th

Peter watched Valerie sleeping. She was truly lovely. No pretense, no botox, nips or tucks. Her body in her mid –forties was hers, not altered, and it was just fine. Peter felt he was fortunate to have Valerie as a mistress. They had a long history as high school friends, neighbors, and now lovers. She was a good woman and she was his.

Peter rolled over. It was one o'clock Friday morning. He should really call Laura. He did not like her home alone since Gloria was away and it was the maid and the gardener's night off.

The suite at The Plaza had a phone in the bathroom. He went in there to call so as not to disturb Valerie. He punched up his home number and got a voice message from Betsy, Laura's friend, saying that Laura was staying with her for the night. Betsy's voice sounded strained. Peter did not like what he heard. His peaceful mood was broken.

Silver Birch Spa
Friday, May 8th

It was two a.m. and Gloria woke shaking and perspiring. Her head was spinning and every part of her ached. She thought she had the flu. Sleep would cure her, she thought. She took two sleeping pills and woke again at seven feeling slightly better, but very unsteady on her feet.

The LaGrange Home
Thursday Night, May 8th

Chris LaGrange parked his Lexus convertible in the driveway and entered the house through the kitchen door. The house was dark except for a low light from his father's den. He realized as he approached the stairs outside the den door that the TV was creating the light. His father must have fallen asleep watching some sports program.

A trifle unsteady from the night's activities, Chris brushed against a table between the den and the bottom of the stairs. The large vase of flowers on the table moved, and in trying to catch the vase, Chris created a noise that woke his father.

"Who's there?" a sleepy voice croaked.

"It's only me, Pop. I'm on my way to bed."

"What time is it?"

"Eleven-thirty," Chris lied.

"No, the TV says one-thirty," responded Vincent, now thoroughly awake. " Where have you been?"

"I told you when I was leaving …at a party at Chad Hawthorne's."

"Why did you lie to me about the time?" By now, Vincent was out of his chair and in the hall. He turned on the bright light that was at the base of the stairs. "Now I know why you lied. You look smacked. What have you been doing? Your eyes are dilated and you smell of beer. Is it just drinking or have you been taking drugs?"

Unfortunately, now Chris's nose started to run. "You have been snorting drugs! I can see it in your appearance," he yelled. "Get to bed. I'll talk to you in the morning. You are not to leave this house until we talk."

Vincent LaGrange had just been dreaming about his surrogate mother/aunt. Vincent's real name was Logrosso. He was born in Bath Beach Brooklyn into an Italian immigrant family. His father, Mario, worked in construction, and was reputed to be connected. He supposedly was a "made" member of the Bath Beach Boys, a Brooklyn gang in the middle of the last century.

There was mob-related trouble in the mid-sixties. Mario disappeared while working construction on the Verazzano Bridge that connected Staten Island with Brooklyn.

Meanwhile, Anna Marie, Vincent's mother, was struggling to feed five children under the age of seven. Antoinette, Marie's sister, married a stock broker, William LaRoche, and moved to Plandome, Long Island in the late 1950's. Antoinette remained barren, and asked her sister if she could raise the oldest, Vincent. Anna Marie reluctantly agreed, but stipulated that Vincent must keep the Logrosso name.

Antoinette made a special effort to have Vincent blend into the Plandome scene. When Vincent arrived on Long Island, she had a speech and etiquette coach work with him. His "dese, dems and dose" were quickly replaced with proper articulation. He no longer dropped the final "R" so "lata" and "afta" became "later" and "after."

Within a few months no one would ever imagine that this well-spoken youngster was just recently removed from playing stickball in the streets of Bath Beach. Vincent's "Brooklynese" and his background had disappeared completely.

As a small boy in the Logrosso family he had been cuffed, beaten and abused by his real father. In escaping to the LaRoches, his life had taken a different turn. Vincent had been treated as a loving member of the LaRoche family. He repaid them by studying hard and achieving the honor of delivering the Valedictory address at high school graduation.

He realized during his high school years that the name Logrosso would be an impediment to his future career. Before he registered at Rennsaleer Polytechnic Institute, Vincent visited the courthouse in Troy, New York. At that time he made arrangements to legally assume the name LaGrange. Vincent Logrosso disappeared from the face of the earth and the newly minted Vincent LaGrange emerged.

From that time on Vincent never looked back. He was a straight A student and well-liked by his contemporaries. The coeds loved his curly black hair and engaging personality.

At RPI he was introduced to the wonders of computer science and electronics. After graduation he started his own computer business. The computer business took off and Vincent's company with it. He was very hardworking and successful.

Vincent dated many women, but none interested him until he met Valerie Braddock, a book editor with an old money pedigree from Westchester. They married when Vincent was in his early forties and their son, Christopher, was born a year later. Vincent kept no contact with his Brooklyn family other than reading newspaper articles about his baby brother, Carlo, a hard worker who had his own successful plumbing business in Westchester.

Vincent sat into the early morning hours pondering how to handle this, the latest incident of his son's misbehaviors. He saw little of the boy as he grew up. Vincent was always busy with the business. He left the raising of their boy to Valerie whom, it seems, was not up to the task. Vincent expected her to be responsible for the boy, but now he realized that Chris had needed a firm father's hand early in life. Valerie was too soft to raise a boy alone and he, Vincent, had left both of them alone to tend to business. This must change.

Where was Valerie tonight anyway? Gone to New York to a book publishing convention. She should be home with her family. It was time for a change in the LaGrange household.

LaGrange Home
Friday, May 8th

Chris collapsed on his bed without undressing. He was exhausted. The problems of the day, plus too many beers and a snort of coke had left him spent.

Looking back on the party, Chris was greatly relieved when Officer Morrissey arrived. He did not have to push the snort. He had a perfect reason for not keeping his part of the deal. But he had tried some at the party to give himself courage before he offered it to others.

The reaction that it gave him was frightening. He felt out of control. He did not like that feeling. He was glad the powder was gone. Finally, Chris rolled over on his bed and fell asleep.

He was awakened at seven by his father who told him to get dressed for school and be downstairs in thirty minutes.

Chris staggered into his bathroom and let the shower beat reality into his brain. His life was a mess. He actually tried to hook his friends on drugs. What an asshole he was. He dented his new car and got involved with drug dealers. He was failing economics and might not graduate, and now his father whom he feared and adored was very pissed at him. He must pull himself together. He must grow up and face reality. While all this was going through his head, he got himself ready and went downstairs.

Vincent was waiting in the kitchen. The table was set with coffee, juice, fruit, cereal, eggs, bacon and toast. Martina, the housekeeper, knew how to start the day. Vincent motioned his son into the chair opposite his and looked straight into Chris's face.

Chris looked down.

"Don't do that to yourself, Chris. Be a man and look back at me," Vincent encouraged. Chris looked up at his father and two pairs of identical dark eyes met.

"Chris, I'm not going to harangue you about your behavior last night. What's done, is done. Let's have a new beginning. Let's talk about the future."

This opening surprised Chris. He came to breakfast in dread and fear. Here he was offered a chance to do better. That was great, but what was going on with his father?

Vincent continued, " People grow up affected by what is around them. In your case, you were deprived."

Chris laughed. "I have everything, Dad. I'm not deprived. I live in a great house with servants. I drive a cool car. I wear the most 'in' clothes. How can I be deprived?"

Vincent went on in all seriousness. "You were deprived of me."

Chris sat back in disbelief. "You were here, Dad."

"Not really. I turned up for dinner a few nights a week. I was good for gifts and vacations, but I was never involved with you. Did I ever go to one of your football games? Did I attend any of the plays you were in at school? Did I ever talk to any of your teachers? Do I know your friends or where you hang out? You know the answer to these questions is NO. Do I love you? Yes. Do I know you? No."

"You were deprived of me, of my involvement in your growing up to be a man."

Chris was stunned. His father was right, he was distant from Chris, but to hear him admit it was amazing. Chris did not know what to say. He had so many problems: drug dealers, car damage, failing grades and now this revelation.

He could not speak, but he felt his eyes fill up as he grasped the table for self-control. Vincent took a deep breath and poured Chris a cup of coffee. "It's not too late, Chris. I'm changing my ways. I want us to be father and son and not strangers." He took Chris's hand that was reaching for the cup and held it. Chris could feel himself relax. He felt safe.

Chris broke the ice by saying, "I hope you don't expect me to take you with me to the Pizza Palace when I meet the guys."

Vincent smiled. "No, but for a while I'm putting some constraints on you so you'll think about your behavior last night. Using drugs, drinking and lying are not appropriate actions for you to take. I want you to promise me, NO DRUGS ever again." Chris nodded, inwardly relieved.

"Control your drinking and never drive when you are drinking." Chris sighed and nodded. Vincent looked at Chris and said, "I want trust between us and that means no lying."

Chris was coming out of his shock, but he felt relief. He was getting something he never had before, his father's attention.

"Dad, you're laying a lot on me at once. I'm overwhelmed. I'll really try to do what you want, but I do need my independence."

Vincent smiled. "You're sounding more like a man already."

Chris moved to his father's side and hugged him. Vincent did not hesitate to hug him back. "Now, Chris, I mentioned some constraints to help you to think about last night and to help you realize that I am in your life and I am there for you. So here goes. You have no use of your car for two weeks. I plan to be home today so I will drive you to school and pick you up. No faces, please." Chris nodded.

"Your social activities will be greatly curtailed. I know you have final exams coming up, so its time to hit the books. That's it. Work with me and together life will be better." Chris agreed and felt at long last that he had a dad and things would get better.

Drummond Home
Friday, May 8th

Betsy dropped Laura at her home at seven a.m., after calling Peter to find out if he would be there to meet her.

Peter grabbed the phone when it had rung only once. He had been home pacing the floor for hours. He saw Laura's cell phone on the entrance table so he knew he could not reach her on that. He did not call Betsy's home when he got her message because he did not want to disturb her family. All Peter did since he got home was walk and worry.

When he heard Betsy's car pull into the driveway, he rushed to the door. Peter was so relieved to see Laura that he hugged her on the front porch like he would never let go.

"Where were you?" Laura asked, her voice muffled against his shoulder.

"With some guys I knew from college. God, I was worried about you. Are you OK?" Peter held Laura at arm's length to look her up and down.

"Fine, for a kid who was abandoned," she said, teasing him.

"You know I would never abandon you and neither would your mom. We love you. What happened last night, anyway?"

"Wild teenage party," she teased again. "But all is fine today."

"Laura," Peter said as they entered the house. "Let's spend the evening together. Mom's away at her spa and we could go out to a nice dinner and a movie. What do you say?"

Laura was thrilled. She rarely got to spend time with her dad, what with his working on his investments and his golf. To be fair, she also had a busy life, so a chance to spend some quality time with him sounded great.

Silver Birch Spa
Friday Morning, May 8th

Gloria knew what was wrong and it was not the flu. She could not deny the truth any longer. It was her recent surgery.

Something was really wrong. She must get home and soon. She rang for assistance and when the manager arrived at her suite, she explained that she was feeling very poorly and needed to be driven home.

Silver Birch anticipated every need, so arrangements were made, for a price, to have one of the gardening staff drive her to her home in Westchester in her own car.

With the assistance of a maid, Gloria got dressed and packed. By nine o'clock, she was departing from Silver Birch.

The manager, while expressing great concern, was happy to see her leave. A sick person at Silver Birch would be a depressing sight and the Spa's goal was to relieve depression.

Gloria nodded off during the drive home, waking now and then to rattling shivers and soaking sweats. Her driver, a strong-looking, swarthy fellow did not speak, but beat time on the steering wheel to the music on her Bose car radio. When they reached her home, he took her luggage to the door and helped her out of the car to join her bags, and then waited to be paid. Gloria gave him whatever cash she had and he seemed satisfied and left.

Peter, exhausted from being up all night worrying about Laura, had fallen asleep on the family room sofa. He was awakened by the sound of a car door slamming. Looking out the window, he saw Gloria's car in the driveway and a large young man helping Gloria out of her car. She looked smashed.

She was supposed to be at a spa, not out carousing, he thought. That guy with her does not seem like her type, but you never know.

Peter walked to the front door and opened it. Gloria almost fell on top of him. Over her shoulder he could see that the guy was halfway down the driveway walking briskly. Grasping Gloria under the arms, Peter gazed into her face and realized that she was sick, not drunk. She could barely stand. Peter got her into bed and had the housekeeper bring her some broth. Gloria was too weak to swallow. All she wanted to do was sleep. Peter left her alone.

LaGrange Home
Friday Afternoon, May 8th

Vincent sat in his favorite chair in his den. He was thinking of his breakfast with Chris. The kid was so much like him, warm and wanting on the inside, but showing a cool self-reliant face to the world. He felt a lot of hope for Chris, but the next few years would not be easy for either of them, especially with Chris away at the University of Arizona hoping to be a walk-on for football.

Now came Vincent's next decision. His relationship with Valerie was not what it should be. Valerie was bright, naturally beautiful, sexual and neglected by her husband. He put his work before both his son and his wife. He broached change with Chris, now he must talk to Valerie.

As he waited for her, he thought of their life together. They married when Vincent was forty-two and Valerie was twenty-eight. He was immediately attracted to her. She was a no-nonsense person, not impressed by his money or position. She had her own money and a good idea of who she was. The first year was all that it should be. Exotic vacations, midnight dinners, sexual adventure all culminating with the birth of their son. They doted on Chris and felt that he was a gift to them.

Valerie was a very involved mother, to the point that Vincent sometimes felt left out. As the years passed, Vincent spent more and more time with his business, forcing Valerie to raise Chris on her own. Valerie's part-time job allowed plenty of time for Chris, and she enjoyed raising him. She liked to see him happy and indulged his whims.

Looking back, Vincent realized it was wrong to have her the sole one responsible for their son. He now regretted those lost years. "Where is Valerie?" he muttered. It was two o'clock in the afternoon. She should be back from her overnight book conference by now.

The fourth time he looked into the driveway, her car appeared. He heard her enter the house through the kitchen, and he left the den to greet her.

Valerie was dressed in a dark business suit with a shawl collar and fitted skirt. The green blouse under it brought out the color of her eyes. She looked very corporate as she opened the refrigerator for a drink.

Valerie jumped when Vincent called her name from behind her in the doorway. She did not expect to find him at home.

"Is everything all right?" she sputtered. "Is Chris OK? Are you sick?" she continued.

Vincent smiled as he came forward to give her a hug. She was stiff in his arms, from fear and guilt, thinking of last night's rendezvous with Peter.

"Everything is OK. I took the day off to spend time with my family and to find out if my subordinates could run the business without me. Although it's into the afternoon and this is the first time I've seen you today," he gently remarked.

Valerie was surprised by his desire to be with his family, and by his chiding her for her absence. This behavior was very unlike Vincent.

"We had a morning session at the conference and I left right after lunch." She would have said more, but she did not want Vincent questioning her time schedule.

"That's great that you want to spend time with us," she smiled.

"But next time, give some notice and I'll adjust accordingly." This was said sincerely not defensively. Valerie cherished the memory of their early married days. She would like to have them back.

"Valerie, I would like to tell you about my plan to change my life," said Vincent.

Now Valerie was scared. Was he putting her on? Did he suspect her affair with Peter? Did he have another woman? What was he going to tell her?

"Vincent, let me make a pot of coffee and we can sit and talk. I'm surprised that you took the day off, and now you say that you are going to change your life. I need time to absorb this."

Vincent laughed, hugged her, gave her a friendly kiss and said, "Don't be concerned. This is good news. But I can't talk now, I have to pick Chris up at school."

"I knew he was hurt. Why didn't you tell me," she exploded.

Vincent looked at her lovingly and smiled. "He's fine, but I've denied him use of his car for a few weeks."

"Why? What happened?"

" Don't worry. He's fine. The problem has been taken care of. I'm here to help you raise our son."

She was flustered.

He smiled again. "Now I'm here for you both." Vincent left twirling his keys around his finger.

Valerie sat at the kitchen table in uneasy disbelief. Her thoughts were running wild. Was Chris in legal trouble? School trouble? Then her thoughts shifted. Did Vincent know about Peter? In a way Valerie was relieved. She had wanted to break it off with Peter and thought their rendezvous at the Plaza would be their last. They had their month long fling and soon would be found out. Maybe they were found out! She went to her desk and called Peter's private cell phone number. She got him on the first ring.

"Hi , what's up?" Peter asked in a rather distracted voice.

"Peter, Vincent is talking about changing his life. I don't understand what he means, but I think we should not see each other for awhile, just to be safe."

"Look I can't talk right now. Gloria came home from the Spa very sick and I'm trying to find a doctor for her."

"Oh, I'm really sorry. I hope she feels better soon."

"I have to get a doctor. We'll talk in a few days." Peter hung up.

Valerie stood there looking at the receiver in her hand. She did not know what to think. Peter was certainly upset. She doubted that what she had said to him had registered in his mind.

Well, she thought, I've warned him of this change in Vincent. There's no more I can do. I do hope Gloria will be all right. I'll bet this illness is a result of her recent cosmetic surgery. She did look pale at the fundraiser Wednesday night, and she did have us leave there earlier than usual saying she was tired.

Too much was happening at once. Valerie needed to calm down and think. She went into the great room and poured herself a large Chardonnay. Taking the drink with her, she went upstairs and took a shower and changed into a paisley sweater and blue slacks.

Vincent returned with Chris and the two of them spent the afternoon going over ideas for Chris's economics project.

High Ridge Country Club
Friday Afternoon, May 8th

Jim headed for the driving range. He had just received a reminder call from Hank to pressure him to eliminate Connie from the tournament. This was the opportunity for Connie to be sabotaged. "How can I possibly do this to Connie," agonized Jim. "She's done the most for Ann than any doctor has ever done."

Connie was already there, having hit a bucket of balls to warm up. "I've started to have a bit of a hook, Jim. We need to get that corrected before tomorrow. Wouldn't you know I'm in Hank's foursome. I really want to beat that shit, pardon my expression."

"Connie, I had nothing to do with the placements. The foursomes were determined by everyone's handicap. You also have Chip Nelson and Peter Drummond in your group. Your 'mental' game is good. Hank shouldn't be a bother. Now let's see what we can do to straighten out that hook. The first hole is a dogleg right, and I want you to start out with a birdie or par. By the way, I brought out a new driver for you to try--it's the latest Calloway and should add five or ten yards to your length."

Jim handed Connie the demo, and she smacked the first ball 225 yards. The second and third balls went even farther. "You've sold me, Jim. Charge my account."

"I'll have to let you use the demo for now, Connie, and order a new club. I notice you didn't hook the driver. Let's try a six iron."

Connie pulled her six iron from her flowered Datrick bag.

"Colorful bag, Connie. Brand new?"

"A gift from my brother, Jim. Now that he's made the pros he likes to give his little sister wonderful presents. Of course, I need eyeshades with this bag."

"I didn't know your brother made the pros--which team?"

"The Giants--he played semi-pro first, but they liked what they saw. Isn't it funny, I'm this tiny little thing and he's tall and hulking, almost like we had different parents. By the way, I can get you tickets on the 50 yard line. The perks of brotherhood."

"Thanks, Connie, we'd love it. Now to some serious business. Take a few practice swings without hitting the ball. Then address the ball for me, Connie."

Connie swung a few times and then went through her pre-swing routine slowly. She gripped the club, took her stance and then put the club head next to the ball. "The first problem is that your club head is closed. Before you take your grip lay your club head next to the ball so it's not turned in. Right. Now take your grip. Then I've noticed you are coming over the top. Your stance and shoulders are too open from the start. That's better."

"You are also coming over the top because you are taking the club back too inside. You need to take the club up straighter. Swing again for me. Perfect. Now let your lower body unwind first. That's it. Hit a few balls for me, Connie." As Connie split the middle of the range, Jim clapped. "You've got it. Do that tomorrow and you're on the team."

"Thanks, Jim. You're a great teacher. What do I owe you?"

"Nothing, Connie. I'm looking forward to those Giants tickets."

"That was a great lesson, Jim. Thanks for straightening me out. Will you be out on the course tomorrow?"

"'I'll be on the first tee at 7:30 when your foursome tees off. By the way, who's your caddy?"

"Sean, Peter's caddy, is carrying double. It was funny. Peter came up to me yesterday and asked if I would like to share Sean with him. He's the best caddy at the club, and so I jumped at the chance. He has such a good eye for reading the greens which is my weakness. I'm surprised Peter didn't ask Hank or Chip."

"Something's going on there, but I don't have the skinny as yet." Jim put the demo in Connie's bag and said, "Don't forget to take the other driver out. You don't want to get caught with 15 clubs."

"Thanks, Jimmy. In my excitement it might not have dawned on me that I was carrying two drivers. I'll remind Sean in the morning. Right now I'm going to stay on the range and try both drivers again."

"Are you coming to the cocktail party tonight? I hear a lot of side bets are going to be made for the tournament tomorrow."

"Yes, my brother Jason is going to accompany me. I don't want to enter the den of wolves by myself. Besides I love your wife. I'm looking forward to seeing her."

"Ann won't be there. She feels self-conscious whenever there's a party and dancing. She uses the excuse that she has to keep an eye on Betsy, but I know it's because of the wheelchair."

Connie took Jimmy's hand and looked him in the eye. "You tell Ann I expect to see her tonight. Don't take no for an answer. Tell her that her doctor advises a night with friends is good for the blood pressure."

Connie was very satisfied with the way she was hitting the ball after her lesson. Her hook had straightened out, and the new driver gave her added distance. She was required to play from the white tees, not the red, while the men were teeing off from the blues. She knew the men would outdrive her, but she hoped her short game would equalize the situation.

Connie entered the ladies' locker room and opened her locker.

She decided to take a quick shower, but just then her beeper went off. Connie dialed her service and found an urgent message from Peter Drummond to call him. Connie sat down and dialed Peter's number. "Hi, Peter, it's Connie. What can I do for you? Our tee off time is 7:30 a.m. if that was what you were calling about."

"No, Connie, I'm in need of your services. I don't know if you've heard, but Gloria went to Costa Rica for some plastic surgery. She came back not feeling well, and we have no family doctor. Could you possibly get her in to see someone. I don't really want to take her to the emergency room. We could wait for hours and she needs some medical attention now."

"Peter, let me make a phone call and get back with you."

Connie dialed Dr. Johnson's office. When the receptionist heard Connie's voice she went to find the doctor. A few minutes later Ben got on the phone. "Ben. It's Connie. My friend's wife had some plastic surgery in Costa Rica, and I think she's developed a problem. Could you see her?"

"Connie, for you I'd fly to Costa Rica to see your friend. Send her right over. I'm almost through with office hours, but I have paper work to do."

Connie immediately dialed Peter who picked up on the first ring. "It's Connie again. My friend, Dr. Johnson, will be happy to see Gloria. His office is in the medical building at Fourth and Main. If you have any medical records from Costa Rica take them with you."

Connie hung up her phone and headed for the showers. She thought to herself that it was crazy to go out of the country for surgery unless you didn't have the money. As Connie took off her clothes she mused, maybe I'm just assuming the Drummonds have money. They live the good life, but so do a lot of people who overextend themselves. She turned on the shower jet and let the hot water course over her body.

As she soaped herself all over she wished that a man's hands could be doing the same thing. Her dates seemed to be few and far between. Ben said she was too picky, but she thought maybe she just intimidated men. As a cardiologist she had to be very confident, and this didn't always sit well with her dates. I'll probably end up an old maid. Maybe better than having a man support me.

Turner Academy
Late Friday Afternoon, May 8th

Laura was opening the door of her "Bug" when Chad called to her across the school parking lot.

"I'll call you later and we'll do something," he yelled. Chad did not even wait for an answer, he just drove away with some teammates..

Laura was still upset about the activities at Chad's party the night before. She resented that he took her for granted. He did not even say goodbye when she left with Officer Morrissey. Now he yells to her that they're going out. Well, she thought, I don't think so. I'm spending the evening with my dad. Mr. Chad, I have a life, too.

When Laura got home, she was surprised to see her mother's car in the driveway. Hurrying into the house, she heard her dad on the phone asking for a doctor. Laura looked around, but did not see her mom. She went upstairs to her parent's bedroom.

She heard a soft moan through the door. Laura opened the door slowly and saw her mom propped on pillows and very pale.

"What's the matter?" Laura gasped as she strode to the bed.

"I feel awful," replied Gloria. Laura could see her mom's usually well-cared for hair stuck to her forehead with perspiration. "I'm shivering and hot and my abdomen is very sore."

Just then Peter entered and went to Gloria's side saying, "I've located a doctor. We have to leave now."

Peter paid no attention to Laura other than saying, "I don't know when we will be back."

Laura looked at Gloria and said, "I hope you feel better." Then she left the room.

Laura was concerned about her mother, but she, herself, felt awful. First Chad takes her for granted, and then her father ignores her. Doesn't anyone recognize that she, Laura, has feelings?

Feeling sorry for herself, she called her friend Betsy and told her story. Betsy said, "Let's go for a pizza. Pick me up around seven and we can talk."

"Sounds good to me," said Laura. "See you then."

Just as she hung up, the phone rang. It was Chad. "Hey, let's go for pizza later," he said.

"I've already planned to do that."

"Oh, have you?" he replied.

"Yes, I'm going with Betsy."

"Great, I'm going to ask Chris to come with me. It will be a foursome." Chad was getting into the party mood.

"Chris has to know that Betsy is a nice girl, not a bimbo," Laura warned.

"Yeah, yeah, I'll tell him. Maybe things will work out that you and I can end the evening together," he remarked hopefully.

"Whatever," Laura replied and hung up. She wished Chad would think of her feelings and wishes and not of his sex drive. The only time he did show interest in her was where sex was concerned. Laura was resigned to thinking, I guess I've got to work with what I have.

Dr. Johnson's Office
Late Friday Afternoon, May 8th

Peter and Gloria stepped out of the elevator in front of Dr. Johnson's office. Gloria clutched Peter's arm as though she might faint. "Hang in there, Glory, we're almost in the office."

Peter's pet name for Gloria was Glory, but he hadn't used it in quite awhile. He remembered how he used to tease her when she wanted to stay in bed all morning. He called her "My Morning Glory" which eventually became shortened to Glory. Where had our affectionate joking gone? he wondered. Between my investment projects and Gloria's committees, we rarely see each other anymore.

Peter opened the door to the office, and they walked into a charming room filled with antiques. It seemed more like a living room in someone's home except for the receptionist's window.

"Mr. and Mrs. Drummond, please follow me. We'll have you fill out the necessary paperwork later." Dr. Johnson's nurse put them into a waiting room.

"Peter, I never should have had more plastic surgery. My last doctor said he wouldn't see me anymore if I did. I didn't listen. Now we're seeing someone we don't even know. If I weren't so sick, I wouldn't have put us in this mess right before your tournament."

"Don't worry, Gloria. This doctor has an excellent reputation according to Connie Carson. He'll fix you up."

Just then Dr. Johnson walked into the room. He shook hands with Peter and Gloria, then asked what was going on. "Dr. Johnson, this is my sixth round of plastic surgery. I had liposuction plus a tummy tuck. I've never felt this awful after any of my other surgeries."

Dr. Johnson took a very detailed medical history from Gloria, and then examined her closely. "Gloria, I believe you have cellulitis. Your temperature is 102 and you are very red and tender around your incision. I recommend we hospitalize you, start an I.V. antibiotic, and run some further tests. I can call the hospital right now to get you admitted." Dr. Johnson started to pick up the phone.

"Wait, Dr. Johnson, could I discuss this with my husband before we do anything?"

"Certainly, I will give you some privacy, but I really feel this is the only way to go." With that, Dr. Johnson left the room.

"Peter, I'm in charge of a huge fundraiser on Sunday, and it will be impossible to get a replacement now. My co-chair had to go to Paris on unexpected business, and I told her it was alright. If Dr. Johnson pumps me full of antibiotic I should be OK by Sunday. Then if I'm not better I'll go into the hospital."

Peter looked at Gloria and wondered what to do. If she went into the hospital now he wouldn't be able to play in the golf tournament, and he would be a dead man. But then, Gloria was his wife. "Gloria, the doctor advises hospitalization. Are you sure you want to disregard his orders?"

"Call him back in, Peter. My mind is made up. I've had infections before associated with my surgeries and I was fine with antibiotics." Her adamant approach relieved any guilt Peter had about playing golf. He left the examining room to inform Dr. Johnson.

The doctor walked into the room. "Peter says you've come to the decision not to be admitted. I strongly advise you to reconsider, but you are the patient. I can't force you. At the very least I'm giving you a very powerful antibiotic which you must start immediately."

"Thank you, doctor. On Monday if I'm not better I'll let you admit me."

"O.K., Gloria, please fill out the papers so I have a good history. If anything more happens, I'm on call this weekend. My new partner is actually trying to qualify from his club for this big money tournament."

As the Drummonds left the room Peter was less stressed. At least he didn't have to confess his severe money problems to Gloria.

LaGrange Home
Friday Early Evening, May 8th

Valerie dismissed the housekeeper for the evening and set about preparing Vincent's favorite meal, osso bucco and risotto. As they were eating this early dinner, the phone rang. It was Chad telling Chris to get down to the Pizza Palace because Laura was going to be there with her friend Betsy.

Chris returned to the dinner table saying, "Dad I'm supposed to meet a nice, smart girl tonight at the Pizza Palace. I think I should go. She could be a good influence on me and be a real help with my economics project. The school paper just did a story on her as President of the Economics Club."

"Chris, you should be a salesman. OK, I'll have Jackson drive you there, but it's an early night," Vincent said in a serious manner.

As soon as Chris left, Vincent invited Valerie into his den for a talk. Valerie was ready for a confrontation regarding Peter, and prayed it would not happen.

"Valerie," began Vincent as he settled in his chair and she sat on a nearby sofa, "the time has come for us to reevaluate our lives."

Her stomach knotted.

"I am no longer a young man. I'm sixty-one years old." Valerie looked at him and noticed the tired lines on his face and around his eyes. She had not looked at him closely in a long time.

"I'd like to make some changes in our lives. I plan to retire within the year."

Valerie could not believe what she was hearing. Vincent's business occupied him day and night for eighteen years and now he is leaving it. Her face must have reflected her thoughts because he smiled and addressed her unasked question

"No, I'm not sick, but I am smart. Working these hours has taken a toll on our marriage and to a far lesser degree on my health. I want to live a long and happy life with you. I won't give that up for my business. We have tons of money, more than you can imagine. Valerie, help me to enjoy the years ahead of us."

Valerie started to cry, from relief and happiness, She got up and sat on Vincent's lap and embraced him.

"I'm a very lucky girl," she said. Despite her dalliance with Peter, she had been lonely for Vincent.

After a while, Vincent broke her mood. He pushed her back so he could see her face and said, "I want to talk to you about Chris." She stiffened, afraid of what she'd hear.

"Oh, he not hurt or sick. You saw him at dinner. Physically he's fine. But he has problems. The thing that made me make my decision about stopping work at this time was something that happened last night."

Now Valerie returned to her seat on the sofa to focus entirely on the conversation and not be distracted by being held.

"What happened," she whispered afraid to hear the answer.

"He came home late and lied to me about the time. That's kid stuff, but he had been drinking and driving. Then I discovered he had snorted some drugs."

Valerie's heart froze. She could not breathe. This was a parent's worst nightmare. "What's going to happen?" she croaked.

"I'm going to do what I should have done years ago. I'm going to act like a father. We will help him through this, and please God, he'll mature into the fine young man he's capable of being."

"Do you think he'll need rehab?" she queried.

"Not yet. I don't think that he is addicted, but Chris is irresponsible. I plan to set some limits and rules for him so he can learn to be more mature."

"Vincent, is this my fault? I did my best. I love him so. I could never deny him anything." She started to cry.

"It's not your fault. We both are to blame. You did too much, I did too little. I'm hoping these next two weeks will give him time to think about his life and how he can control his destiny."

Valerie nodded. "I'll do all that I can. I'm so happy we are helping him together."

High Ridge Country Club
Friday Evening, May 8th

It was six o'clock and the orchestra was tuning up when Jimmy headed for the bar. "What'll it be, Mr. L?" asked Louie the bartender. Jimmy alternated between his southern taste for "Wild Turkey" and the country club choice of Grey Goose on the rocks.

"A double Wild Turkey for starters, Louie. I think this is going to be a long night."

"Some Kickin' Chicken it is, Mr. L. I think I'm going to be busy tonight. I had Jack come on just in case. I hear the betting is going to be pretty heavy. Is Mrs. Lawson here tonight? She always has the sunniest smile."

"My daughter is going to bring her over soon. Ann seems to tire easily these days. Fridays she has hydrotherapy which seems to add to her tiredness, but I know my wife wants to see the outcome of the betting. I think she's placing some of her own money on Connie Carson."

"That's not a bad bet from what I hear, although the scuttlebutt is that a woman shouldn't be on the team."

"She's a member, Louie, and has the same right as any man to qualify."

"I have nothing against women, Mr. L. Just passing along what I hear. Oh, by the way, Mr. Drummond called and said he couldn't be here tonight. Something about his wife being ill. He definitely wanted you to know he will be playing tomorrow."

Just then the orchestra swung into "My Satin Doll", and Babs Nelson came over to claim the first dance with Jim.

"Come on, Jimmy. You know Chip has two left feet. I don't understand why he doesn't have better coordination being such a great golfer." She held out her hand to Jim, and he whirled her onto the dance floor.

Jim tried to be accommodating to the members' wives since it was good for business, and Ann encouraged him to be as social as he wanted. He especially enjoyed dancing with Babs as her five feet ten inches melded nicely with his six foot two inch frame. With her blonde hair flowing down her back and legs that didn't quit she was a real stunner. Most eyes were on the twosome that looked like they were Arthur Murray professionals. Of course, a few catty members whispered that it was inappropriate for Jim to be having so much fun dancing when his wife was in a wheelchair.

Babs looked much the same as she did fifteen years ago when she met Chip at the Italian restaurant where she was working. Not of country club background, Babs's actions were not always perceived positively. Sometimes members joked that she was NOOC(not of our class).

Hank cut in which was perfect timing as Jim needed to set up the betting boards. First, however, Jim detoured to the bar again to refresh his drink. "God, he's going to be plastered before we even start the preliminaries," said Hank as he pulled Babs a little closer. He had the hots for his best friend's wife and enjoyed slow dancing with her. Those magnificent tits really gave him a hard on, and he hoped one day to get her into bed or the bushes wherever the chance might happen.

Babs on the other hand was annoyed with Hank because he thought she was an easy lay. She wished she could give him a good kick in the groin. She wanted some information, however, so decided to give Hank a little of what he wanted. It wasn't the first time she had used her body for information. "Jim can hold his own, Hank. I think his drinking stems from Ann being in the wheelchair. You know about the car accident. You were at college with them." Babs ground her body a little closer to Hank and said, "I won't tell a soul, not even Chip. He can't keep a secret."

"Well, if you'd like to adjourn to my Jag think I have what you want, if you get my drift." Hank started to dance her towards the door.

"Oh, Hank," Babs laughed as she pulled away, "We'll miss the betting. Look, it's about to start." Babs went over to her husband's table where unfortunately the Hawthornes were also seated.

Babs never quite figured out why Hank had married Sarah who was almost a recluse. She was well-known for her portraits especially of animals and children. Sarah was Hank's second wife, his first having left for her personal trainer. Babs could understand the choice his first wife, Amy Sue, made although that left Chad, their son, in limbo. Chad never seemed to have much of a home life, drifting between his friends and Hank. Amy Sue had moved out to California with her boyfriend and seemed to be what they called a "surfer girl." Periodically there was talk of sending Chad out to be with her, but nothing ever came of it.

Sarah was olive-skinned, dark-haired and intellectual, the very opposite of Amy Sue. She had a 10-year-old daughter, Stephanie, from her first marriage, just as dark and sallow as her mother. Babs found her personality to be very mousy, but who wouldn't be with Chad and Hank in that household. Hank seemed very proud of the fact that Sarah belonged to Mensa, an organization for the gifted. However, she seemed to lock herself in her studio and work for hours at a time. If the Hawthornes didn't have a housekeeper Babs doubted that either Hank or Chad would have clean clothes or home cooking.

She must be good in bed, mused Babs, although that skinny little body didn't seem sexually appealing. Babs thought Sarah was drab looking, but what saved her was her fantastic sense of style--she would look good in a paper bag.

The word was out that Chad was a druggy--Hank always spouted that "boys would be boys," but Chad did more than the usual teenage stuff. Not that Babs would really know since Chip and she had no children. She was actually happy no babies had ruined her figure, but she knew it was a real disappointment for Chip. Their lack of conception was due to Chip's low sperm count--after years of trying he wanted to adopt, but Babs was too happy with their childless lifestyle. She loved going to Atlantic City and now Foxwoods for gambling, or else Canyon Ranch for a spa treatment which would not be possible with little ones.

All in all it was a pleasant life with Chip, and if she needed a little sexual excitement there were always men willing for a light flirtation. Hank would not be one of them, however!

Chip stood and held out a chair for Babs. "My husband, always the gentleman." Babs turned and gave Chip a big smooch on the lips. That should get Hank going, she thought. "What a beautiful dress, Sarah. You can't go wrong with basic black."

Hank slid into a chair beside Sarah. "I sure know how to pick em, don't I. Of course, you didn't do so bad yourself, Chip."

Sarah eyed Babs up and down. "That red dress certainly is a knockout, Babs. I sure couldn't carry it off, but you do." Sarah did not add that it made Babs seem slightly cheap with its dipping neckline and no back, but she preserved the peace.

Besides, she was hoping to leave soon and concentrate on the Springer Spaniel she was painting. The commission was extraordinary, and she could use the money. Hank was very stingy with what he considered "their" money, and she was hoping to put a skylight in the studio.

Just then Jim had the orchestra do a drum roll. "Ladies and gentlemen, the betting is about to begin. There are twenty players trying to qualify for four spots. Qualifying takes place tomorrow and Sunday. The lowest four players at scratch will make up the team from High Ridge. You place your bets on each individual player. If your player doesn't qualify you lose your bet. That money will be divided equally into the betting pots of the four winners so think about your hunches. Good luck."

"Are you betting on yourself, Hank?" asked Babs

"Sure, honey chile," said Hank. "If you think you're the best, then you should. I see a lot of action by my name. Guess I need to get over to the betting board myself. Don't worry, Chip, I have fifty bucks with your name on it, too."

Chip and Hank strolled over to the board as Ann Lawson arrived. "Am I too late to place a bet?" she asked Sarah.

Sarah and Ann were actually good friends, and Sarah had given Ann a portrait of Betsy for her last birthday. Betsy was like an older sister to Stephanie, and was the Hawthorne's babysitter.

"Ann, so good to see you," exclaimed Sarah as she leaned over to kiss her. "Let's both go over to the betting board. I want to bet on Connie. Do you want to come, Babs?"

"I'm going to finish my martini first. You go ahead with Ann. I do think you're crazy for betting against Hank or Chip though. What will Hank think?"

"Don't worry, I'll place a bet on him, also. I'm not stupid!" With that Sarah pushed Ann's wheelchair over to the betting board.

A group of men were congregated around Jason Carson, some in awe of being so close to a New York Giant player. "What are the Giant's chances this year, Jason?" asked Brad Wellington.

"I think we have a good chance to make the play-offs if everyone stays healthy. The Philadelphia Eagles look strong, but you can't rule out the Dallas Cowboys either."

"Speaking of ruling people out, how do you like your sister's chances?" Hank asked.

"I guess the betting board speaks for itself. She always was a tough little kid and hung in there. And she's conscientious. Connie's not on call tonight, yet she's with a patient. She just called and said she couldn't be here tonight." Jason thought to himself that he probably sounded defensive, but he was tired of men picking on Connie because she was a woman. "I hope she beats their asses," he thought.

Quite a crowd had gathered in the bar near the betting. Five thousand dollars had already been bet on Hank. Then came Chip with four thousand. Peter Drummond and Brad Whitington were tied with three thousand apiece. "What has been bet on Dr. Carson?" asked Ann. She strained to see around the group standing in front of her.

"I can't believe it," said Sarah. "Opposite her name is seven thousand dollars. Many of her bets are from the women," Sarah whispered in her ear.

"Do my betting for me, will you, Sarah?" Just then Jim came over to Ann. Ted, the assistant pro, had taken over for him.

Jim gave Ann a kiss on the cheek. "I'm glad to see you, Ann. Is Betsy here?"

"No, Jim, she's gone to the pizza parlor with Laura. She didn't have to babysit Stephanie because Stephanie has a sleepover."

Jim crouched by Ann's chair and said in a low tone, "I don't like her being with Laura, Ann. You know Laura can be a little wild. Look what happened last night. Her own parents don't seem to care."

"Jim, I don't exactly know what to do. Laura and Betsy have been friends since grade school. We just have to trust Betsy. She's very level-headed."

"Even the most level-headed kid can be swayed, Ann. You know that better than anyone."

"Don't remind me, Jim, I'm living proof of that." Then Ann picked up Jim's drink. "And what is this?"

"I did have a drink when I first came, Ann. Now I've switched to Pepsi. I know I have to quit."

Ann put her arms around Jim. "Please, Jim, don't ruin your life over what I've done."

"Ann, now is not the time. Let's have a long talk after this tournament is over."

Just then Ted announced, "The betting is closed, and everyone should head home for a good night's sleep. The first foursome will tee off at 7:30 a.m. The weather forecast bodes well, the course is in magnificent shape so it should be a great tournament."

"What's this 'bodes well,' Ted?" joked Hank. "I thought you were our golf pro and not a college professor."

"Ah, Hank, I know ya'll went to Wake Forest where they use simple words, but we graduates of Syracuse have to flex our intellectual muscles every now and then." There was good-natured laughter and a spattering of applause.

As people started to drift away Ted said, "Wait, I have a big surprise. The $250,000 prize money put up by the 20 High Ridge entrants will be displayed in a Waterford bowl at the entrance foyer of the clubhouse. Look, but don't touch, however. There will be two guards with big guns standing beside the money."

Everyone started to chatter about this revelation. "Isn't that asking for trouble?" asked Ann. "It certainly sounds like it would be tempting to steal."

"Don't worry," said her husband. "We have Safety Assured guards watching the money the whole time it's on display. Then they take it by armored truck to their vault where it's locked up."

"Money will then be added by the other three clubs as the tournament travels. Guards will always be with the money when it's displayed. Safety Assured has never had a robbery while guarding valuables. We picked them because they had successfully guarded the huge Egyptian exhibit at the Alton Museum."

Just then Brad and Millie came up to the Lawsons. "Hi, Ann," said Millie as she gave Ann a kiss. "Pretty dress." Ann had chosen a pale blue crepe dress that covered her legs. Her hair was in a French twist, and her mother's pearls finished off the outfit. Millie thought to herself that she had never met a woman as kind as Ann. She wished Ann's circumstances were different.

"Millie, you look so pretty, too." Millie had chosen a purple and pink caftan to cover her ever-growing figure. It was bold yet suited Millie perfectly.

Brad clapped Jim on the shoulder. "We're two lucky men, aren't we, Jim?" As Jim nodded in assent Brad also said, "You're doing a great job with this tournament, Jim. I hear it was your idea. By the way, I don't see the Drummonds. He's still competing, isn't he? People have bet on him."

"Yes, Brad, he's in the tournament. He didn't make it tonight because of Gloria."

"It's probably one of her fundraisers. I'm surprised she hasn't roped you in to this one, Millie."

"No," Jim said. "I think Gloria was sick."

"She didn't feel well last Wednesday night. She had just gotten back from Costa Rica, and I think she was having a medical problem," Millie replied.

"Millie, you ever have any plastic surgery and I'll divorce you. I like a woman with natural beauty. I've seen your pretty face for twenty years and I don't want to see another one that looks like a stranger." Millie was secretly relieved. There was much pressure to start with an eyelift or a tummy tuck and continue on. Millie was happy with her plump self. Besides, a round face showed no wrinkles and Brad seemed perfectly happy the way she was. Millie gave Brad plenty of sex, and also cooked his favorite meals. He was a satiated man.

Just then the band leader announced the last dance of the evening. Brad took Millie in his arms, and Hank led Sarah out onto the dance floor. "Sarah doesn't seem very enthusiastic, Brad. I think Hank is a horse's patutie."

"Don't be too hard on Hank, Millie. When you're the sales manager of your company and profits are down you have to talk yourself up a little. You know what egos we men have."

Brad proceeded to do some intricate steps with Millie. For being round of girth she was very light on her feet. Brad pulled her a little closer and whispered something in her ear which made her blush.

Sarah started to pull away from Hank, but he held her firmly and wouldn't let her leave the dance floor.

"Don't they seem like oil and water, Jim?" said Ann as she observed the two. "I really feel sorry for Sarah. He was so attentive to Stephanie when he was first dating Sarah--I think that's what sold Sarah on him. With Sarah a young widow, she wanted a substitute dad for Stephanie."

"I think he might have helped her in her portrait business, too. Hank can be a really nice guy-- maybe Sarah needs to meet him halfway."

Ann, usually the peacemaker, was very blunt. "I think Hank is a 'player,' Jim. He chases anything in skirts and Sarah knows it. I think she has a great deal of disdain for him now, and I don't blame her."

"He might chase skirts, but he never catches them, Ann. It's his good ol' boy southern charm. He makes women feel attractive. What's the matter with that?"

"It's at the expense of Sarah. I think you're playing the devil's advocate with me. Never mind, let's not spoil a nice evening. Take me home and I'll make you a happy man." Jim wheeled Ann out to valet parking as the party broke up.

Lenny's Pizza Parlor
Friday Night, May 8th

Laura and Betsy opened the door to Lenny's Pizza Parlor. Lenny's was the local hangout for most of the jocks at Turner Academy and also Franklin D. Roosevelt High, the public high school. There had always been a friendly rivalry between the sports teams even though they were in different divisions.

Turner was last year's state football champion in Class C, and so was Roosevelt in Class A. Every now and then both teams would hold an unofficial scrimmage for fun against each other.

Lenny's was a cozy restaurant with red leather booths and a huge brick oven which added a cheery glow to the place. A juke box sat in one corner and played not only current songs, but oldies from the fifties and sixties. Elvis Presley songs were a favorite. Usually every twentieth tune was "Heartbreak Hotel."

Laura peered around until she saw Chad and Chris in a back booth. Laura slid in beside Chad and he gave her a kiss. "Hey, Chris," said Betsy as Chris made room for her on his bench seat.

Chris looked appreciatively at Betsy and said, " Lenny's is definitely improving with you pretty girls. I sure got lucky tonight."

"Don't count on getting too lucky, Chris. You're with 'Miss Prude of the Year,'" stated Chris as he put his arm around Laura.

"Let's have a nice evening, Chad," said Laura. "Betsy's my best friend and a lot of fun. You don't always have to be smoking pot to have a good time."

Betsy looked as if she might bolt from the booth. Chris put a hand on her arm and said, "Don't worry, Betsy. We're just here for pizza and cokes. What kind of pizza do you like?"

Chris had never realized how cute Betsy was, with her sandy-colored hair pulled back into a ponytail and prominent freckles marching across her nose. Chris knew Betsy liked to work out, and her figure proved it. Normally Chris liked big-breasted girls with curvy hips, but Betsy's slender body suddenly appealed to him. A nice new challenge, he thought.

"Believe it or not, I like anchovies."

"My favorite, too," Chris said. "Hardly anyone likes it that way. Looks like we're a fit."

Betsy felt a delicious shiver pass through her body. Chris was the actual tall, dark and handsome man found in romance novels. Betsy had seen Chris's father a few times dining at the country club, and except for a few lines of aging , the family resemblance was amazing.

Laura and Chad were having their own conversation when Chris said, "Let's go and play the jukebox. Elvis or Eminem?"

As they walked to the jukebox, Chris cautiously put his arm around Betsy and pulled her close. Normally Betsy would've resisted in such a public place, but surprisingly she snuggled into Chris's body.

As Chad gazed at them he stated, "Who would've thunk it."

"Chad, Betsy's a wonderful person and really cute. Maybe Chris can rise above his usual bimbo."

Chad nuzzled Laura's neck. "There is something Chris wants to rise. The same thing I do," and Chad started to put his hand under her shirt.

"Not here, Chad. It's too public. Wait until later." Laura firmly removed Chad's hand just as the pizzas arrived. Chris and Betsy returned to the table, holding hands. All four happily chatted as they ate their pizza.

"Would you like a ride home, Betsy?" asked Chris. "My dad's chauffer is bringing our limo, and maybe the four of us could go to my home for awhile and watch a movie. We have all the new releases."

"Wow, you have a chauffer, Chris? It must be great to be driven wherever you want to go." Little did Betsy know that Chris's car had been taken away and the only wheels he would have would be the ones driven by someone else.

"Laura has her mom's car so we'll just go home by ourselves," said Chad as he looked knowingly at Laura. "See you at the club tomorrow for the tournament." They scooted out the door as the LaGrange limo pulled up.

"Hello, Jackson," said Chris as the black chauffeur opened the door for them.

"Looks like rain, Mr. Chris," said Jackson, as he started the limo. "I believe your father said you were due home shortly?" Jackson had been a family retainer for years and was part bodyguard and nursemaid to Chris in addition to serving as chauffeur, gardener and handyman. Many a time he had saved Chris from escapades that had turned sour. This gentle reminder was for the curfew imposed upon Chris after the pool fiasco.

Chris did not want to appear that he had to be home at a certain time so told Jackson, "Yes, I know Dad is worried about my economics project, so I promised I would be home early to work on it."

"Chris, why didn't you tell me you had schoolwork. We can see a movie some other time."

"I think we have time to do both, Betsy. I know you do well in economics. Maybe I could pick your brain."

"Chris, what a nice thing to say. I would be happy to help you."

LaGrange Home
Friday Night, May 8th

As Jackson steered the car into the LaGrange driveway, Chris asked him to let them out at the main entrance of the house rather than at their usual entrance, the kitchen door.

Chris wanted to impress Betsy with his home and what could be more impressive than the fan-shaped marble steps leading to the etched glass double doors with boxwood topiary lining the way. Betsy had been to the Drummond home many times, but that was an old house. This home was much newer and had a definite edge. Chris led her through the entrance hall past the formal dining room and living room to the great room at the back of the house.

This room was almost entirely made of glass with a huge marble fireplace at the far end. On one side of the room there were lounge chairs set auditorium style before a large plasma television and a retractable movie screen. Another corner held a work station with an oval conference table and chairs and a computer with all its attachments. There was an area for card playing and another with a coffee table and comfortable chairs for conversation. To the immediate right of the entrance was a wet bar and an enclosed kitchen.

Betsy was astounded at the size of the room. Her whole house could fit in there. Valerie and Vincent were watching a film which they turned off as the teens entered.

"Mom, Dad, this is my new friend Betsy Lawson," Chris said as his parents approached. " Laura and Chad couldn't make it. Laura said her Mom was sick, and she wanted to go home early."

"Great to meet you," said Vincent taking her hand. Valerie stood by smiling approvingly.

"It's good to meet you, too," replied Betsy.

"I understand that you are a very good student," said Valerie. "What is your favorite subject?"

"I love economics," Betsy replied.

"Why economics?" Vincent inquired.

"Oh, I find it fascinating how all aspects of life are affected by money and commerce."

"How did you develop that interest?" Valerie continued.

"Well, it started when my folks gave me an allowance, and I realized that the things I wanted to buy had a variety of prices depending on the manufacturer and the vendor."

"Will you listen to that girl talk?" exclaimed Vincent. "Chris, take this sharp girl with you next time you go shopping."

Chris blushed, saying, "Shopping is the last thing on my mind now. I have to finish my project for economics by Monday or I may never shop again." He ended with a forced laugh.

"Chris, I told you I'd help you with your project. Let's take a look at what you've done so far, and maybe I can come up with some ideas."

"Betsy, I promised you a movie. That's why we're here," said Chris halfheartedly.

"The movie can wait. You're project is due on Monday. Let's get to work."

Chris's face lit up. How lucky can I get? he thought. I'll be able to spend time with Betsy and ace my economics project. "I really appreciate your offer, but are you sure you have the time for this?"

"Yes, now let me see where you are in your research and then we'll take it from there." Upon scanning the notes Chris and Vincent created that afternoon, Betsy reached a decision. "I'm not working tomorrow. So after doing a few chores at home, I'll be able to help you, if you want me to."

Valerie followed this conversation with a happy heart. Here was a nice girl that Chris seemed to like. She was smart and cute and ready to help him with his school work. The answer to a mother's prayer .

"Dad?" asked Chris. "Do you think I could pick Betsy up tomorrow?"

Vincent was a man of his word. Chris was not going to drive until his two weeks of punishment were up. "Your Mom is going to the bookstore in the morning. I can drop her off and pick up Betsy on my was back. That will give you more time with your project. Betsy, what time would be good for me to come to your home?"

"Ten-thirty would be fine, thank you."

"Settled. Tomorrow is economics day in this household," stated Vincent.

"I think I should be getting home," said Betsy. "I want to check some economics notes that I have. They might be helpful."

"Chris, this young lady is amazing," said Vincent. "No problem getting you home, Betsy. I'm sure Jackson hasn't put the car away as yet so he can drive you. Chris, I'm sure you want to accompany your friend home," Vincent smoothly stated.

Chris was thrilled to spend time alone with Betsy in the back of the car, but he also resented not driving her himself. His wiser side prevailed, things were going well, let's not make waves.

"That's good," said Chris as he began to lead Betsy to the entrance.

"It was very nice to meet you. I'm happy to be able to help Chris."

As the two of them walked away, Valerie gave Vincent a kiss on the cheek. She loved him and the way he handled Chris. She knew that things were going to be just fine.

Chris and Betsy got into the back of the town car. Betsy gave Jackson her address and settled back on the soft seat.

Chris, who usually was in command in this kind of situation, sat stiffly in his seat.

"Your parents seem very nice," said Betsy.

He smiled at her and said, "And you are very nice. I can't thank you enough for helping me with this project."

"That's what friends are for," she said smiling.

"I think you are going to become my very good friend," Chris said, taking her hand.

A sudden storm came in from the north and the rain fell in torrents. Jackson drove carefully through the sheets of rain and lightening. In a few minutes they were at Betsy's home.

Jackson got out and brought a large umbrella from the trunk to Betsy's side of the car. She exited with Chris right behind her. Chris took the umbrella from Jackson and said, "I'll walk Betsy to her door."

Jackson smiled, nodded and slid behind the steering wheel.

They picked their way through the puddles and up the path to the modest ranch house. When they reached the door, Chris tipped the umbrella to shade them from view of the street and gave Betsy a chaste kiss.

She slipped inside the house unable to speak. She was thrilled and frightened. No boy had ever affected her like that before.

Lake Mahopac
Friday, Late Evening, May 8th

Laura and Chad drove out to Lake Mohopac in Laura's Volkswagon, a present for her 17th birthday. There were conditions attached to the car, however, mainly dealing with passing grades. Laura did not have an educational interest in school, but enjoyed all the social activities. Her grades were good enough to be on the soccer team, but just barely. Since Laura loved her little "Bug," with Betsy's tutoring help she never lost the privilege of driving.

"Pull into our secluded spot, Laura. I'll get the blanket out of the trunk. There are also a couple cans of beer left from the party." Laura pulled over into a grove of trees near the lake. It was too early for the normal crowd who frequented the lake to heavily pet or have sex.

Laura and Chad settled themselves on the blanket, and Chad took the pull tops off the beer. "To our first night together, Laura," said Chad as he raised his beer.

"I'm scared, Chad," said Laura as she took a big gulp of beer. "I thought I was ready, but I don't know anymore."

Chad pulled out a joint and lit it. "Don't worry, Laura. We'll take this nice and easy." He passed over the cigarette for her to take a puff. "Take a couple big drags, Laura. It will relax you. I promise you, this will be wonderful."

Laura did as she was told and took several big drags plus several swigs of beer. All of a sudden she felt very relaxed. Chad laid her gently down on the blanket and started to massage one breast.

"Take my blouse off, Chad," slurred Laura.

Chad slid his arm under her back and with his other hand quickly unbuttoned her shirt. Laura wore no bra so her magnificent young breasts stood straight up. Chad slowly licked one nipple while kneading the other with his hand. Laura writhed and felt Chad's hardness through his chinos. Then Chad stopped and took off Laura's jeans and panties.

He kissed and licked her navel and then moved his tongue lower. Laura had never experienced such sensations in her life. She did not know if it was the marijuana and beer, but she did not care. Finally Chad reached her special place. He buried his face in her auburn mound while reaching for her breasts with both hands. Laura could not stand the teasing and pushed Chad's face into her body. She came quickly. Chad pulled down his pants, and put a condom on his erect penis. Slowly he slid into Laura's wetness.

"Am I hurting you, Laura?" he panted. He did not wait for the answer, but plunged deeply into her vagina. "Oh, God!" He exclaimed as he felt his release. Chad peppered Laura's face with kisses, and then rolled off her, tossing his rubber into the bushes.

"Laura, are you OK?" asked Chad.

"Oh, Chad, I can't believe it. This is what I've been waiting for all my life."

"Plenty more where that came from. We'd better get dressed and leave now, Laura. The storm is beginning to start and it looks like a whopper. You need to drop me off at my house before going home." Chad pulled up his zipper, buttoned his shirt and handed Laura her clothes.

Disappointed that there was not any cuddling, Laura put on her own clothes. Without any talking both climbed into Laura's car and drove home.

DeAngelo Home
Saturday Morning, May 9th

"Will ya look a dis!" exclaimed Rosie DeAngelo as she read the "Close Up with Collette" column in the Westchester Weekly.

It was Saturday morning and her husband, Angelo, was at the table eating his eggs over easy and hashed brown potatoes. He paid no attention to her. He was reading the sports page which was grasped in his free hand. Their two children were watching cartoons on the kitchen TV.

"I said, look a dis," Rosie insisted even louder.

"Wha?" responded Angelo, never taking his eyes from the newspaper and his plate.

"One million dollars cash is de prize in a local golf tournament! Boy, I'd love to see dose bucks all together in livin' color."

"Wha ya talkin' about?" She finally got his attention.

Angelo snatched the column from her and began to read. "Dose rich fucks must be nuts to leave dat amount of cash lyin' around a club house." He laughed.

"Angelo," said Rosie exasperated. "Watch your language around Li'l Angelo and Anna Marie."

Little Angelo was smacking his cereal with a spoon, keeping time with the cartoon music. Anna Marie, eyes glazed over, was noisily sucking her thumb. Neither seemed affected by their father's language.

"Aw right, aw right, I'm outta here. Today is collection day and da boys will be waitin' for me at the club." He left the table taking "Close Up with Collette" with him.

Neopolitan Club
Saturday, May 9th

Nunzio and Nicky were waiting for Angelo when he arrived. After a brief greeting during which there was much hand-shaking and back-slapping, Angelo showed them the newspaper column.

"Whad a fuckass move! Leavin' all that cash lying out in de open," exclaimed Nicky.

"Just what I thought," said Angelo "…an easy grab."

"Wait, guys," said Nunzio. "We can't do nothin' without talking to Big Carmine. He's our boss and he calls the shots."

"Good," replied Angelo. "Let's tell him about dis when we bring in our collections dis afternoon. Who knows, info like dis might cause him to increase our cut of de take."

The Drummond Home
Saturday, Six a.m., May 9th

Gloria woke early when Peter headed out to the golf course. She wished him well in qualifying for the tournament, but as Peter bent to kiss her goodbye, he could see that she was not any better than the night before.

"Glory, I think I should stay home," he offered.

"Don't be silly. It takes a while for the antibiotics to kick in. I'll be much better tomorrow. You go out there and win. That will help me to feel better."

He gave her hand a squeeze and departed. She smiled to herself and fell asleep.

Qualifying Round
Saturday Morning, May 9th

Hank met Peter's caddy, Sean, in a far corner of the clubhouse parking lot. "Mr. Hawthorne, I know I said I'd help you out but, I'm starting to get nervous. What if Dr. Carson gets the drift of what we're doing? I could be banned from caddying here." Sean furtively looked around.

Annoyed with the caddy's attitude, Hank snapped, "Just look like you're taking my clubs out of the trunk. Then no one will pay attention to us."

"Now I know," Hank continued, "Dr. Carson should have fifteen clubs in her bag instead of the fourteen club limit. I saw her on the driving range Friday afternoon, and she had two drivers in her bag."

"Yes, I just got her clubs out of the bag room and she does have too many clubs. Ordinarily I would tell her right away." Sean shifted uncomfortably behind Hank's Jag.

"Listen, Sean, I know you want that caddy scholarship and it's yours. The committee met last night before the cocktail party. It was between two of you and I made certain you got it. I know you've been accepted to the University of Pennsylvania so it's a full ride provided your grades stay good. Plus here's five hundred bucks from me for your trouble today. Don't worry, Dr. Carson won't fault you. The ultimate responsibility is hers. I'm in her group and I'll make sure she knows it."

Connie arrived early Saturday morning at the club. She wanted to loosen up at the driving range, and finish her practice by chipping and putting. Outside the pro shop she saw a big sign that said, "Driving range closed due to flooding. Imbedded ball rule in effect. You may lift, clean and place the ball in your own fairway."

Connie went into the pro shop to find Jim Lawson. "What is going on, Jim? We can't hit balls before such an important tournament?"

"Sorry, Connie, I even wanted to close the course, but I was overruled. The range is under an inch of water. You know it's the lowest spot on the course. We had a deluge last night. It's the same predicament for everyone."

"You're right, Jim. I just guess I'm nervous."

"You have 30 minutes before you tee off. Practice your chipping and putting. That's where the game is anyway."

Just then Peter walked into the pro shop. "How's Gloria?" asked Connie. "I was worried you wouldn't be able to play."

"Dr. Johnson was wonderful. Gloria's in bed, and Babs is going to look in on her. If she isn't better by Monday she'll be in the hospital. Thanks for your help, Connie. Sorry I didn't call you last night, but by the time I got Gloria's prescription and then got her settled, I knew you'd be at the cocktail party."

"I'm glad she's OK, Peter. I didn't make the party myself because of a patient. I guess we'd better get out to the putting green. We have 20 minutes before tee off." As Peter and Connie went up to the putting green they found Chip, Brad and Hank already there.

"Hi, Connie, Sugar," said Hank. "Shouldn't you be getting your hair and nails done on a Saturday morning?" With that he sunk a 15 foot putt.

"At least I have enough hair to style," retorted Connie. Then she ignored Hank and went to the opposite end of the practice green to putt.

Fifteen minutes later Jim called for the first foursome. Peter, Chip, Hank and Connie made their way to the first tee.

Jim announced, "All USGA rules apply to this tournament. The four lowest scores will advance to the playoff tournament. Good luck to everyone."

"Before you tee off please identify the ball you will be playing. The lowest handicap will tee off first. That's you, Hank. I will be roaming the course in a golf cart if there are any questions during the round. "

Hank stepped up to the tee and drove straight down the fairway 280 yards. Chip followed, but was in the left rough possibly behind a tree. Peter hit a great shot next to Hank's. Then it was Connie's turn. She also smacked the ball down the middle, but not as far as the men. Four golfers and two caddies carrying double marched down the first hole. Connie reached her ball first, marked it, and threw the ball to Sean to clean. Connie was in perfect position for the dogleg right. "Give me my six iron, please, Sean."

Sean handed her the club and said, "Dr. Carson I'm going to leave your clubs here for a minute while I help Mr. Nelson look for his ball. They seem to be having some trouble finding it in the rough." With that Sean set Connie's bag down and went over to where the others were looking.

Connie hit a perfect shot that landed past the pin and spun back to within three feet of the hole. Satisfied, she put her six iron back into the bag and, aghast, noticed that two drivers were in there. Just then Jim drove up to her in his cart.

"Great shot, Connie, I told you I wanted a birdie out of you on the first hole."

"Jim, I have a terrible problem. I just realized I have 15 clubs in my bag. I forgot to take out the extra driver after I practiced yesterday."

"Connie, you go over to help them find Chip's ball. They're so busy, they won't notice me slipping the extra club out of your bag. You don't deserve this problem. I don't know why Sean didn't catch it."

Connie looked at Jim and said, "I know you want to do this for me because of your wife, but I can't let you get involved this way. I'll take the extra two stroke penalty on this hole. It's my own stupid fault for not counting my clubs myself. I always do that before every tournament. Here though, take my extra club with you. A two stroke penalty is all I can handle right now."

Just then Chip found his ball so everyone left the rough. He had to punch out from behind a tree and ended up thirty yards short of the green. Both Peter and Hank put their second shot on the green although not as close as Connie. As the foursome walked down the fairway Connie announced, "I need to take a two stroke penalty . I started out with too many clubs. I gave the extra one to Jim."

Peter turned and looked at Sean. "You didn't catch that?" He asked quizzically.

"Sorry, Mr. Drummond. Phil Michelson started the pros carrying two drivers so I thought Dr. Carson was doing the same thing." Sean hung his head down in disgust. He needed that caddy scholarship because his parents had five other children to support. He had never sold himself out before, and it didn't feel good.

"Don't blame Sean, Peter. As I was telling Jim, it's my responsibility. Let's finish this hole so we don't hold up the group behind us anymore than we already have."

Chip hit his approach shot fat and two-putted for a bogey five. Peter and Hank took pars while Connie had a birdie which turned into a bogey with her penalty.

"OK," Connie thought. "That hole is finished. Now I need to forget it and concentrate on the other seventeen."

For the next eight holes birdies, pars and bogeys were traded among the members of the foursome. The ninth hole ended at the clubhouse. Hank said, "I don't know about the rest of you but I gotta take a leak bad. You must have an iron bladder, Connie."

"I'm surprised you need the bathroom, Hank. You used the woods enough the first nine holes," stated Connie.

"You peeking, Connie? I'll give you a better look if you want it. We have another nine holes to finish first, however."

"Save it for Sarah--she's your wife, remember?" As they walked through the pro shop to the men's and ladies' locker rooms, Peter gave a low whistle.

"Look what is just outside the pro shop--our prize money, all 250,000 dollars in a big bowl."

Chip spoke up. "Yes, and there are 'big' men guarding that 'big' bowl. Look at all that money."

"This is going to cause quite a sensation," Peter said. "I imagine there will be quite a crowd once members know it's here. Wouldn't you just love to run your hands through all that green?"

Just then the starter poked his head inside. "Your foursome has five minutes before you're on the tenth tee." They quickly finished inside and headed out.

Hank asked Chip, "Have you heard how the group behind is doing? That's our competition."

"I hear Brad had three birdies on the front. I don't know about anyone else. What do you think about Connie and the clubs?"

Putting for the Green

"I think it's too bad she found them on the first hole. It would've been one less person to worry about," grumbled Hank.

They drove their carts up to the elevated tenth tee. "Well, here we go again. Good luck, everyone," said Peter. His thoughts were that he had better be the one with luck. Peter teed off and hooked it perilously close to out-of-bounds.

"I'd better hit a provisional--it's a Nike with a 'P' on it." His next shot went straight down the fairway.

Peter headed with Sean to where his first ball had stopped. The others went to their balls. Peter's ball was extremely close to out-of-bounds. "What do you think, Sean? In or out." Peter had always been very good to Sean, giving him large tips and helping him to apply for the caddy scholarship.

"It's your call, Mr. Drummond. I could see you hitting it and calling it in. I'll back you up."

Peter lined himself up between the two out-of-bounds stakes. He knew if any part of his ball was on the imaginary line between them he was out, and that would add two strokes to his score. "I need that prize money so desperately," he thought. Quickly, before he did the wrong thing, he picked up his ball and said, "It's out." He then walked over to his provisional.

"I can't believe he called it out," said Chip to Hank. "It could've been called either way."

"One more for our side, Chip. Don't knock it."

Peter was now lying three. He took a nine iron, hit the pin and the ball went into the hole. "A routine par," Connie laughed. "Shot of the day."

Hank shook his head. "When it's your lucky day at golf, you can do no wrong."

Nothing major happened for the next seven holes. The eighteenth hole was the most treacherous on the course. It was a severe dogleg left with a brook running across the fairway just before the green. Long hitters could take a shortcut over the trees. If you took the straight fairway shot you had to use an iron. Then the green was severely elevated so you couldn't see what happened to your shot.

Both Peter and Hank sailed three-woods easily over the trees. Then Chip stepped up, adjusting his glasses. "Telltale sign he's nervous," whispered Hank.

Chip hesitated about what to use. Finally he pulled out his 3-wood. Taking the club back too far, Chip tried to compensate and hit the ground before the ball. It took a dive right into the middle of the trees. There were mutual groans, but nothing said. Chip trudged with his caddy right into the middle of the forest. They immediately found the ball nestled in the crook of a tree.

Chip said, "I'll have to take an unplayable." He measured two club lengths not nearer the hole and dropped his ball.

Dave, his caddy, said, "You have a clear opening to the green."

Chip fiddled with his glasses again as he studied the situation. "I'll have to hit a good solid shot, but I can do it." Chip felt comfortable with his stance and took an easy swing. Unfortunately the ball hit a couple leaves which stopped its momentum enough that it fell into the middle of the water. "I'm done," Chip said to Dave.

"Don't give up now, Mr. Nelson. A chip and a putt will give you a six." As they headed out of the trees Chip saw that Hank and Peter were on the green in two, and Connie was just over the brook.

Chip dropped a ball behind the water and thought, "A six will give me a double bogey. I can't get a seven." He took out his lob wedge and put the ball eight feet from the hole. By now quite a crowd had gathered around the green. Many had come to cheer on the players, but there were also those who had arrived for the free cocktails and hors d'oeuvres. Everyone had come to see the money.

Connie received a big round of applause when she put her ball within two inches of the hole. Hank and Peter both missed their birdie putts--now it was Chip's turn. Dave and Chip studied the putt from both sides of the hole. "I think you need to keep it in the cup, but on the left side." Dave then moved out of the way.

Chip thought maybe the putt broke a little more so played it a ball outside the hole. It just slid past. The four finished and walked off the green.

There was a huge board outside where the players could record their scores. Hank had the lowest score, a 74. Then came Peter with a 75 and Connie with a 77. Chip was last with a 79.

The second group came in very unhappy. "That rain last night really killed us," griped Brad Wellington. "The conditions were abominable."

Putting for the Green

Jim came out of the pro shop. "We're due shortly for another downpour. I need to speak to you, Hank."

As they walked back into the pro shop Jim said, "If we get the same downpour as we did last night, I'm going to definitely close the course tomorrow. The superintendent has said we've already damaged a couple of the greens. Hank, I think this is going to be a one day tournament. You're the president so you make the decision. I think many of the entrants are going to be pissed."

Hank thought about it for a minute. It actually seemed to his advantage to make this a one day tournament. All the scores in his group were decent. He hadn't seen the second group's scores, but they didn't sound good. The rules for this tournament even stated that it could be a one day tournament if the course had to be closed for any reason. The only downside was that Connie would be part of the foursome. I have to admit she did play well, and we want the best in order to win the million. Her cute little shape would be great to look at, too. "OK, Jim. Make the announcement."

Hank decided to stay in the pro shop so it wouldn't look like he had made the decision. All five groups had finished, and were gathered around the board. The liquor had started to flow. A jovial atmosphere prevailed until Jim walked in with his pronouncement.

"Are you kidding me? I put up $12,500 just to play for one day?" protested one of the men in the last group.

"Forget it," said another one angrily as he stalked off

"Don't get mad at the pro," said Brad. "It's stated in our rules that this could happen."

"Easy for you to say, Brad. You'll be in the final four, if we can't play tomorrow."

"Look guys," said Connie. "It hasn't happened yet. Don't get upset until we see the weather forecast."

"It's already starting to rain," said Chip as he looked outside. Brad had beaten him by one stroke, that missed putt.

Hank came out of the pro shop and looked at the board. He couldn't believe it when he saw Brad had beaten out Chip. He put his hand on Chip's shoulder. "Maybe we'll still play tomorrow."

High Ridge Country Club
Saturday, May 9th

Everyone trooped upstairs to either drown their sorrows or toast their good playing. A group of spectators had crowded around the Waterford urn to gape at the cash inside it.

"Sir, please step away," said one of the Safety Assured guards to an onlooker. "You are closer than five feet to the money." The guard's hand started to slide closer to his holster.

The onlooker put his palms out and said, "I'm backing off, sorry." Peter slipped away to call Gloria. He got Babs on the phone. "How's my wife feeling?"

"She's been sleeping most of the afternoon. Her temperature is still up, but she's only had 24 hours of the antibiotic. Laura's home so I'm going to leave now. Keep your cell phone on so she can reach you if necessary. I'm coming up to the club--are celebrations in order for Chip and you?"

"Thanks, Babs, you've been great. Chip is in fifth place right now, but he can make it up tomorrow. I'm second, but that can change, also. I'm heading home so you can tell Laura."

Babs hung up thinking that the Nelson household would be an unhappy one tonight. "I guess I'll run up to the club and have a few drinks to get me through the evening," she decided. As she opened the Drummond front door a huge bolt of lightening flashed through the sky. Babs made a dash for her car, but was soaking wet before halfway there. "Thank goodness I have some dry clothes in my locker."

By the time Babs entered the side entrance of the clubhouse both the money and the guards were gone. As she started to enter the locker room Hank turned the corner. "Someone looks like she needs some dry clothes. You're still awfully cute dripping wet."

"I'm going to take a quick shower and change my clothes. Could you tell Chip that if you see him?" As she opened the locker room door it was pitch black. "Hank, could you turn on the light before you go back up? I'm not sure where the lights are."

"Sure, honey, I do my best work in the dark. I'll have the lights on in a jiffy for you."

Hank found the light switch and left. Babs shed her wet clothes and stepped under a jet of hot water. She let it run over her body until she warmed up. The shower became very steamy. Babs reluctantly turned off the spigots and pulled back the curtain. She started to scream until she saw who it was. Hank was standing in front of her with a terrycloth robe in his hands.

Babs quickly closed the curtain. "Are you crazy? You're in the ladies' locker room. What if someone walks in?"

"Here, sweetheart, let me help you on with the robe. I knew you were cold, so I found this for you. I was just going to drop it on the bench and leave, but you finished too soon." Hank turned his head as he held out the robe for her to slip on.

"I'd really like to believe you, Hank, but somehow your innocent face isn't so innocent."

"Here, at least let me dry your hair--it looks so cute unruly." Hank took a towel and started to rub Babs's head vigorously.

"That does feel good, Hank," said Babs as she leaned back against him. "Keep rubbing."

"I could rub somewhere else if you'd like, Babs."

"I think that might get us into a lot of trouble, so scoot. I don't want to explain to anyone why I'm half-dressed. Babs grabbed the towel from Hank and started to dry her own hair.

Hank turned her around and slowly pulled her towards him. He kissed her hard on the lips and thrust his tongue in her mouth. At the same time he slipped his hand into her robe. Just as he felt her rounded breast she pulled away and said, "You've taken advantage, Hank. Chip's your best friend. Now get out."

"Then don't be a tease, Babs. To be continued later." With that Hank winked at her and sauntered out.

LaGrange Home
Saturday Morning, May 9th

Valerie smiled across the breakfast table at her husband. They were having a leisurely breakfast and reading the newspapers. Chris was already at the computer, working on his project.

"I can't believe the change in Chris," said Valerie. "He seems focused and relaxed."

"He's growing up." responded Vincent as he dipped a biscotti in his Cappuchino.

"That Betsy seems very nice. I hope he hangs on to her."

"The LaGrange men know good women when they see them and he is like his Dad." Vincent winked.

Valerie laughed and returned to the Westchester Weekly. Her eye was drawn to the picture at the top of the gossip column, "Close Up with Collette." There was a great picture of the five friends at the function at the Metropolitan Museum last Wednesday.

They looked so happy and so elegant. Valerie was surprised as she read the accompanying story that the focus was on the million dollar golf tournament and not on the fund raiser. Collette went into great detail concerning the fact that the prize money was to be in cash and was to be displayed in full view at each of the matches. Two hundred-fifty thousand would be added to the prize as the tournament traveled from club to club ending with the full one million at the final match at High Ridge.

Valerie felt that all Gloria's work on the fund raiser was slighted in favor of the golf story. She was sorry that Gloria did not get the full credit that she deserved.

Bookstore
Saturday May 9th

Vincent had dropped Valerie at the mega chain bookstore in town and promised to return in a few hours to take her to lunch. Valerie wanted to look at some of the books she had edited and gather information on how they were selling and to whom. She also wanted some time alone to call Peter and find out how Gloria was doing. She reminded herself not to say anything about Collette's coverage of the fund raiser.

Valerie called the Drummond household and got Laura. "How's your Mother doing?" Valerie asked.

"About the same," Laura muttered.

"Is there anything I can do to be of help?"

"No, thanks. She's on medication and we just have to wait."

"How are you and your Dad doing?" Valerie ventured.

"OK, Dad's in the qualifying tournament today."

"Right. I forgot about that."

"Well, he didn't," Laura snapped.

"I'm sure that's what your mother wanted him to do."

"I guess."

"If you need anything , just call."

"That's OK, Mrs. Nelson is coming over in a few minutes."

"Good, it's not easy to be a caretaker all alone."

"Don't I know it," said Laura and hung up.

"It's going on noon," thought Laura, "and Chad has not called. After last night, you'd think he would. And he knew my mom was sick.

Chad can be very self-centered." With that thought, Laura banged her hand on the kitchen counter knocking the phone off the charger.

Vincent picked up Betsy as planned, and she chatted away as he drove her to the LaGrange home. Normally, Betsy was on the quiet side, but she was so happy, she could not stop herself from talking.

Chris met them at the door and the two of them went directly to the computer. Martina, the housekeeper, had left sodas and sandwiches nearby. She knew teenagers were always hungry.

Chris gave Betsy a warm hug and said, "I can't thank you enough for helping me. If this project is not an A, I'm in big trouble. You are a great person and really cute." With that, he kissed her on her pert nose.

Betsy thought she was going to faint, but pulled herself together and smiled up at him. Taking a deep breath, she began to explain to him how the use of a variety of graphs would make his project more effective. The two of them worked about two hours without a break.

So intent were they on their work, that they did not see a man in the outside greenery looking in at them. He noted that they seemed to be alone and smiled his big gap tooth smile. He had given this kid one thousand dollars of cocaine, street value, and got no return.

He heard from Chad yesterday, when he came for his weekly weed that the police had come to the pool party. He could not believe that Chris had dumped the blow. Chad said that Chris had no choice but to do it. Gap Tooth was still out one K. This kid was in debt to him. He knew where Chris lived because he checked the registration that was in Chris's car when it was repaired. Gap Tooth decided to pay Chris a visit and discuss the debt. He went around the house to the front door and rang the bell..

Vincent opened the door, and Gap Tooth was surprised. He thought that the kids were alone. He had to think quickly. "I'm here checking your lawn sprinkler system. Is it working OK?" he asked, creating a cover story.

Vincent, who was rarely involved in the running of the house, knew of no watering problem, so he called Chris.

As Chris and Betsy approached the front door, Vincent moved aside and Chris saw Gap Tooth. Chris gasped. He had desperately hoped his relationship with this guy was over. Now Gap Tooth was standing in the entrance of his home next to his father.

"Wh, what's up ?" Chris managed to stammer.

"This man wants to know if we have a problem with our landscaping sprinkler system?"

"None that I know of," replied Chris faintly. "Maybe he has the wrong address."

Hearing this comment, Gap Tooth gave a house number. It was for a home six doors down the street. "Sorry," said Gap Tooth. "These fancy houses don't always have their numbers nice and clear." He walked away.

Vincent shrugged as he closed the door on the departing stranger. Chris and Betsy returned to the computer area where Betsy began to analyze the graphs she had created. Chris was glad that she was occupied and did not notice that he was worried. He toyed with some statistics as he tried to gather his thoughts. Gap Tooth was definitely looking for him. Why? To get Chris to push dope? To get money for the cocaine Chris destroyed at the pool party? To hurt Chris for dumping the drugs?

Any way he looked at it, Chris knew that he was in trouble. He needed to avoid Gap Tooth . Chris vowed never be alone where he could be taken captive and hurt or worse. Ironically, he was glad he could not use his car for two weeks. This way he had to have someone with him when he was out of the house.

As he was considering his plight, Vincent entered the room and announced, "It's two twenty. I'm going to the bookstore to pick up your mother and take her to a late lunch."

"Oh my gosh," said Betsy jumping up from behind the computer. "I must get home. I promised my Mom that I'd do a million chores for her and I'm late."

"I'll drop you off on the way to the book store," offered Vincent.

"That's great. Thanks."

"Wait a minute," said Chris. "I'll go to the book store with you. I need to buy The Economist and look at some other sources. Besides, I can't allow my economics consultant to go home without my walking her to the door." He smiled and Betsy blushed.

"OK, we leave now," said Vincent.

When they arrived at Betsy's house, Chris helped Betsy out of the car and took her hand as they walked to the door. He looked in her eyes and said, "I must finish this project this weekend and I could use more help, if you have time for me."

Betsy blushed and said, "Tomorrow afternoon might work out."

With that, he kissed her on the cheek and said, "I am a very lucky guy. I'll call you later." Then he bounded to the car where Vincent was waiting.

Valerie was waiting outside the bookstore when they arrived. "Have you put me on a diet," she teased. "I expected you thirty minutes ago. I'm ready to eat."

"Chris and Betsy have been working on his project all this time, and they seem to be doing well with it," replied Vincent.

"To hear news like that takes a slight edge off my appetite. Where are we lunching?"

"Mom, I'm staying here to work some more."

Valerie raised her eyebrows in surprise and smiled. "Is this my son, the scholar?"

"Not quite, but I do have work to do."

Vincent broke in with, "We'll be back in an hour or so. See you then." Valerie got into the car and they drove away.

Chris entered the bookstore and headed for a spot where he could use his cell phone. Maintaining an upbeat appearance was exhausting him. He had to talk to someone about his situation before he freaked out. He punched up Chad's cell phone number and after a half dozen rings, Chad answered.

"Chad, I must talk to you," he whispered.

"I'm kinda busy right now. I'm at Charleen's, and her parents are not home."

"Chad, I'm in big trouble."

"Chris, I'm in big sex," and Chad hung up.

Chris looked at the silent phone and began to shake. What was he going to do? How could he get out of this awful situation?

High Ridge Country Club
Sunday, May 10th

It was 6 a.m. and water stood in puddles around the club. Jim met Seth, the greens keeper, outside the pro shop. "I guess we had the same idea," Jim said. "I already know the answer to my question, but is the course playable?"

Torrents of rain came tumbling off the awning above the pro shop door. Jim went inside to deactivate the alarm system and realized it was not working. Periodically with lightning and rain the system seemed to short out. The alarm company was always out trying to fix it. Jim personally felt it was not worth the money to keep it. The alarm company owner was a member of the club so Jim had to tread lightly.

"Sorry, Jim, but I'm firm on this. Most of the course is under water. There is flooding in the town next to us. This course will definitely not be open today. You'd better start calling the members." Just then Ted Rankin walked in.

"Seth, I just heard you say the course was closed. Jim, you've been here nonstop for the past six days. This is supposed to be your day off. Why don't you go home and I'll call the members. No one is going to come out in this downpour."

When Jim left the house, Ann was peacefully asleep under the covers. He thought it sure would feel good to climb back in bed and spend a cozy morning with her. Betsy would be gone babysitting Stephanie so we would have the house to ourselves. I could even make my famous French toast. Of course I would have to leave the bourbon out of the maple syrup. That made it my signature dish. But no more.

"Thanks, Ted, if you have any problems with the members give me a call. I do need a break." Jim put his umbrella back up and ran to his car. As he drove away, he realized he had forgotten to tell Ted about the alarm. I'll call him when I get home, he thought. The prize money is locked in Safety Assured's vault so that's OK.

Now he was very anxious to get back to Ann. This tournament was getting to be too much for him. The finals will be at our course with a cocktail hour and dinner to follow. What a headache. Plus all that money just sitting around. Even with the guards it was an uncomfortable situation.

Ted started calling all the members. He had listened to the answering machine first, and found that most of the members who did not think they would qualify had already called and withdrawn. "Dr. Carson, this is Ted Rankin. I have some very good news for you. You have qualified in third place for the team. More information will be given out Tuesday."

In answer to Connie's query, Ted told her that Jim had gone home possibly sick. Ted said he had promised to call everyone for Jim. Ted suggested that he would be willing to do a clinic for the team. No, it wasn't Jim's idea, but his own.

Ted finished calling the other three team members: Hank, Peter and Brad. They had all agreed to meet Tuesday afternoon for a clinic. That evening the four teams would meet at High Ridge for the first time to be given the tournament format.

After Ted's call Hank surmised incorrectly that Jim was on a toot and had turned over his pro duties to Ted. Ted seemed to be handling this responsibility ably. Hank wondered if Jim had noticed that his contract had only been extended for one more year. Based on Jim's drinking, the Board was adamant that a change could be forthcoming.

The Lawson Home
Sunday, May 10th

Jim opened his front door and walked into the foyer. He took off his raincoat and shook out the umbrella. Buddy, Jim's old hunting dog, came padding across the floor, wagging his tail. Even though Buddy was retired Jim could not bring himself to buy a new dog. As it was, Jim couldn't remember the last time he had been hunting. Why would he need a new dog? Jim patted Buddy's head as he tiptoed into the master bedroom. Ann was still asleep. Her silky blonde hair lay across the coverlet and she was breathing softly.

Jim took off his wet shoes first and then his clothes. Quietly he slipped in beside Ann and nuzzled her shoulder. Ann turned and said, "Jim, I thought you had to be at the club?"

"The tournament got cancelled so I thought I'd come back and have a morning in bed with you. The coffee's made and I can bring some juice, too. I stopped at the drive-in for donuts. You pick a movie and we'll pig out."

"Oh, Jim, we haven't done this in so long. Remember how every Sunday it would be our ritual?" Ann turned and curled up in Jim's arms.

"Ann, you pick the movie and I'll be back with the food."

He kissed the top of her head, threw on a robe and went to the kitchen. Betsy had grabbed a yogurt and was walking out the door. "Leaving for babysitting, Punkin?"

"Yes, Dad, Sarah's doing a family portrait and they wanted her to start early. I'm going to make a big breakfast for Stephanie, and then we're going to the mall. Sarah's letting Stephanie buy a pair of shoes."

Jim reached into the cookie jar where they kept emergency money and handed Betsy a fifty. "Here, buy yourself a pair of shoes, too."

Betsy came over and kissed her dad's cheek. "Thanks, Dad. I saw a great pair of platform shoes at Nine West."

"Are those the kind of shoes that are so high you can fall over?"

"Dad, I've never heard them described that way, but you have the concept. Can I use your car instead of Mom's?" Ann's car was equipped with special controls so Betsy usually tried to take her father's car.

Jim threw her the keys. "Your Mom and I are going to have breakfast in bed and watch old movies. Be careful out there, Betsy. It's really slippery. You have your cell phone if you need to reach us."

"Oh, Dad, I'm not a little kid. See ya." Betsy walked out the back door. Then Jim remembered to call Ted, and gave him the information about the alarm.

Then Jim took the donuts out of the bag and put them on one of the good China plates. Chocolate-covered cake ones were Ann's favorite. Jim liked the gooey Boston cremes. He put the coffee carafe, mugs and creamer on the tray. Last came two goblets of juice. Jim carried the tray into the bedroom and placed it on the bed between them. "Wow, if you weren't already married I'd marry you!" joked Ann.

"What movie did you pick?"

"I thought maybe we could have that nice talk you mentioned at the cocktail party. You can start with any juicy gossip."

"O.K., let me take a bite first." The custard came squirting out of the donut as Jim broke it in half. He took a big swig of coffee and said, "Let me see, where should I begin. First, your doctor is one of the four team members. Second, you won $500 in the betting pool. Third, I love you."

"First, I'm so glad Dr. Carson made it. Second, I have my eye on an antique table. That $500 will make it mine. Third, I love you, too."

"O.K., Ann, now we get down to the serious business. We have to talk about 18 years ago. You have to get over it."

"Jim you have to get over it, too. I know it's why you drink so much."

"Ann, I quit drinking Friday night. I had my last Wild Turkey. I pledge to you I'm going to remain sober. It's for you, but it's also because of my job. I'm slightly worried that Ted is becoming more popular than I am."

"Everyone thinks you're a great teacher, Jim. And look how well you organized this tournament. No one could do it better than you." Ann had finished her first donut and reached for a second.

"Hey, that's mine. I guess I'll have to settle for a jelly."

"You just love anything that has filling. Now that the donut situation is settled let's clear the air. We've been living under a cloud for too many years. Let's start with the fact that at the Sigma Chi party we had a terrible fight about getting engaged and you got stinking drunk."

"Ann, you know I loved you then, but I wanted to try and get on the pro circuit. That wouldn't have been any life for a wife."

"I told you I already had a teaching job lined up. I could've joined you on holidays. Every family has hardships."

"I don't think hardships include sleeping in your car because you don't have the money for a motel room."

"If you love each other you manage. We could have done it. Then I was so impulsive. I wanted to go home, and I stupidly accepted a ride from one of your fraternity brothers." Ann started to cry.

Jim put the tray aside and gathered her in his arms. He buried his face in her hair and pulled her close. "I should have stopped you, but I was too mad and too drunk. I knew the guy you went with had been drinking. I should've called you a cab."

"I should've known better, Jim. He seemed sober enough to drive, and I wanted to make you jealous. I really just wanted to get out of there. What a stupid mistake. The guy misses a curve and drives right into a tree, killing himself. When I woke up in the hospital I was paralyzed. End of story."

"Not an end to the story," Jim said tenderly. "I was with the doctor when he said you were pregnant and that you might lose the baby. Why didn't you tell me you were pregnant?"

"I was going to tell you that night, but then we had the fight. Thank God I held on to Betsy. Of course, then you couldn't go on tour. I felt awful."

"It was alright, Ann. I wasn't good enough to make it. Deep down I knew it. I just thought it would be my last chance at having fun before I took on responsibility. Hasn't this worked out for the best? We have a beautiful daughter and a fulfilling life."

"How fulfilling can it be if you have to drink to get through the day? Often I've thought how much better off you would be without me."

Jim tilted her face up and gave her a kiss. "You are my life, Ann. This stupid drinking is just a habit. I'm done. We've come so far. You have a whole new career as an interior designer. Your appointment book is filled. I look around our home and it looks like it should be on the cover of House Beautiful. I think that's why you're such good friends with Sarah---you are both 'artsy craftsy.'"

"Did you see the wonderful mural she just did in the dining room? I feel like I'm actually in an Italian vineyard. I think I'll have her start on your den next," Ann teasingly said.

"You know my den is off limits. Only golf paraphernalia allowed!"

"Oh, Jim, I'm so happy. I see the pitying looks people give me sometimes, but I couldn't have a more fulfilling life with my family and profession. Maybe it was a lesson I had to learn." Ann reached out and caressed Jim's cheek.

"O.K., enough . This emotional talk is hard for me to do," Jim admitted. "Let's get out the movie--what about Tootsie. I need some humor."

The Drummond Home
Sunday Morning, May 10th

Gloria woke early, feeling slightly better. She did not dare to get out of bed. She must save her strength for this evening's fund raiser.

Peter felt her move and opened one eye to look at her across the pillows. He smiled and stroked her cheek. It was still very warm. Her fever must still be high. He rolled over and turned his thoughts to yesterday's qualifying round. He was still amazed that he scored so well. He was on his way to winning the money he needed to pay his debt to the mob.

The phone rang , interrupting his thoughts. It was Ted Rankin informing him that the course was closed, and that Hank, Connie, Brad and he would represent High Ridge at the first match in two weeks.

Peter could not believe his luck. A rain out! Now he really was on his way to the tournament prize.

He told Gloria the news as she was taking her medication. She smiled at him and said, "Good news brings good news. I feel a little better. By tonight I'm certain I'll be well enough to host that party."

In her heart, Gloria knew that she was not better, but she felt driven to fulfill her obligation. Besides, the antibiotics would kick in and then she would be OK.

Laura also woke early. But then, she really had not slept. Chad never called her. All day Saturday, she waited. She never heard from him. How could he treat her this way? After what they did Friday night? Was she just a convenience? An easy lay?

She hated him and to a degree she hated herself.

Peter stayed home for the day anxious about Gloria's health. She seemed determined to host the fund raiser. He did what he could to get her to take some broth at noon time, but she had little appetite.

When he returned to the kitchen with Gloria's tray, he found Laura sitting at the counter drinking chocolate milk. She was still in her pajamas and she looked awful-- tired, drawn and her hair needed washing.

"What's up, Baby?" he asked.

"Nothing," she muttered and started to leave.

Peter took her by the arm and looked at her. "Your mom will be OK, don't worry."

"I'm not worried," she snapped. "She'll be fine, she always is."

Peter did not let go. "Laura, let's try to be a family and not go our separate ways. Let's pull together. Mom and I could use your support this evening." Letting go of her arm he continued, "Mom is determined to attend this fundraiser. She's not up to it. We must be there for her. Will you please come with us? It would mean a great deal to both of us."

Laura looked at him for a long time and thought that it would be nice if someone would be around to support her once in a while, but she said, "If that's what you want, OK, I'll go, but I don't plan to enjoy myself. I'm going to, as you said, 'support' Mom this evening. By the way, I don't have anything appropriate to wear tonight. You will have to give me a charge card so I can buy a dress." With that she left the kitchen.

Peter looked after her. Something is wrong. Laura was usually pleasant with him. She saved her snippy remarks for her mother.

Gloria lay in bed planning her preparation for the party. She'd get up to shower and wash her hair at five o'clock. Her hairdresser was expected at five-thirty to do Gloria's hair and make up. Gloria decided to wear her empire style chiffon sapphire gown. The dress style would cover the bandages that Dr. Johnson had placed on her oozing incision. She had to remember to keep that area dry in the shower.

By six-thirty, she'd be ready to leave. Cocktails started at at that time. She could miss the first twenty minutes. She had used this hotel for many other functions. She knew the Banquet Manager was attentive to detail so she need not worry about seating, flowers, music, etc. He could handle it all very well. But, she had to be there as chairperson for the evening. She had to welcome everyone graciously, especially the big donors.

The dinner was scheduled for seven-thirty to be followed by the art auction. All she had to do was make opening remarks before dinner and introduce the auctioneer after dinner. That should be an easy evening, but in her heart, she knew it would be difficult. She felt weak and disoriented.

It was time to get out of bed. Gloria felt very sore when she rolled onto her side to get up. When she stood up, her legs were shaking. Somehow she got into the shower. The warm water revived her and she was robed with her hair wrapped in a towel when the hairdresser arrived.

An hour's work found Gloria's blond hair wound into a sleek French twist. The makeup worked magic to hide the dark hollows under her eyes and the drawn look of her face. Her dark blue eyes were sparkling (from fever), and they looked even larger, reflecting the color of her gown. Gloria selected large drop sapphire and diamond earrings to complete her ensemble. The total effect was perfect. Few guests would be able to detect how sick she was.

Peter, Laura and Gloria got into the car without husband and daughter noticing that she was ready to collapse.

Gloria smiled at all around her at the hotel's entrance and settled herself on a sofa in the cocktail area. Her head was swimming and her vision was blurred .

She had trouble remembering the names of those who greeted her. She felt cold, but was perspiring. The guests were in a festive mood and did not notice Gloria's distress. They were distracted by the large crush of people, the exotic drinks, the hors d'oeuvres and the loud music.

Soon it was time for dinner. As the guests sought out their tables, Peter and Laura escorted Gloria to their seats. Peter noted that Gloria was shivering.

"I'm fine," she smiled and sat down heavily. Laura came out of her bored mood to notice that her mother's brow was wet with perspiration. She handed Gloria a hankie.

"Are you all right, Mom?"

"I'm just fine and very happy to have you here."

It was time for Gloria to go to the podium. Peter took her arm and mounted the steps with her. He stood just behind her to one side as she grasped the sides of the lectern for support.

Gloria gave the audience her best smile. They quieted down and she began to speak. Her voice was hoarse and breathy.

"Thank you for coming to this event. Your presence here makes it a success. We are here… this… evening…" Everything was getting black and Gloria started to fall backwards. Peter caught her. The audience was stunned at what was happening.

The maitre'd stepped up and calmed the crowd while Peter half-carried Gloria off the stage, and with Laura's help laid her on a sofa. Gloria was unconscious. A waiter gave Peter a wet napkin which Peter placed on her forehead. Laura was patting her mother's hand. The next thing they knew, EMS had arrived and Gloria was on her way to the hospital in an ambulance.

The Hospital
Sunday Evening, May 10th

The ambulance with its siren blaring, pulled up next to the emergency room. The paramedics lifted the gurney carrying Gloria out gently and wheeled her through the doors. She had been hooked up to an IV and was moaning softly. Several minutes later Peter and Laura came roaring up to the entrance.

"Laura, take the car and park it. I'm going in to find your mother." Peter ran inside and tried to go in the treatment area. A burly guard stopped him and asked what he was doing.

"They just brought my wife in by ambulance. I have to see her. She's really ill."

"If they just brought her in, it will be a while before you can go in there. Why don't you step up to that window on the right and the receptionist can help you." The guard stood solidly before the doors in case Peter tried to go in.

"Excuse me, but my wife, Gloria Drummond, just came in by ambulance. What do I have to do to see her?"

The receptionist shuffled through her papers. "I have nothing on her yet, Mr. Drummond. The ER doctors will be examining her. In the meantime we need to have you fill out some information on your wife. If you'll just go through the door across the hall the triage nurse will ask a few questions. By the time you're done with the paperwork, you should be able to see your wife."

As Peter approached the triage area Laura came up to her father. "How's Mom?" she asked.

"I haven't been able to find out, Baby. I've put in a call to Dr. Johnson's answering service. They are trying to locate him. Let's go in and talk to the nurse and maybe we can find something out."

Peter and Laura went into the office and filled out the forms needed to admit Gloria. Then they were told to sit in the waiting room and they would be called.

Laura cringed and shrunk closer to her father. A young man covered with tattoos was holding a blood-soaked cloth to his ear. A woman across the way had terrible sores on her leg.

"Dad, this place is making me sick."

Just then Dr. Johnson walked into the room and motioned Peter over. "Hello, Mr. Drummond, I was actually in the hospital when my service found me. Your wife is being admitted now, and should be in a room shortly. I'm sorry she didn't enter the hospital last Friday. Her temperature has spiked to 104 and the redness and tenderness have spread. She's already been started on IV antibiotics, but the cellulitis has really taken hold. If she isn't any better by tomorrow I might put her in Intensive Care. Both my partner and I will be making rounds tomorrow."

Laura came up to her father. "Dr. Johnson, this is my daughter, Laura. Laura, Dr. Johnson." Laura put out her hand and shook the doctor's.

"Please, can we see my mother now? She seemed awfully sick when she was put in the ambulance."

"Come this way." Dr. Johnson ushered them past the guard and into the treatment area. The ER was so busy that gurneys with patients were lined up in the hallways. It seemed like doctors and nurses were everywhere. The tattooed man walked in followed by a policeman. Dr. Johnson pulled a curtain back and there was Gloria hooked up to an IV, and the wires attached to her body were running to machines.

Gloria smiled faintly. "Oh, Mom," Laura said in anguish as she held Gloria's hand. Peter went to the other side of the bed and kissed her. Just then a nurse walked in and told Dr. Johnson that his patient would now be moved to the fourth floor.

"I advise you both to go home and get a good night's sleep. Visiting hours are over and we need to get your wife settled. Hopefully she will sleep well--I'm going to prescribe a sleeping pill. Nothing heals more than a good rest."

Peter looked at Gloria. "Do you mind if we go home? I'd like to get Laura settled. She has school tomorrow." Gloria nodded her head so they started to leave.

Dr. Johnson walked out with them. "Both my partner, Dr. Williams, and I will be in to see her tomorrow. I'm giving her a heavy dose of antibiotics. Hopefully that will knock the infection out. Visiting hours aren't until noon, but you can come earlier if you wish." Peter thanked the doctor, and put his arm around Laura as they walked to the car.

The Drummond Home
Monday Morning, May 11th

The next morning Laura popped her head into Peter's bedroom. "Dad, do I have to go to school today? I'd really like to see Mom."

Peter had just finished dressing and was ready to head downstairs for coffee. "I want you to go to school, Laura. I'm going to spend most of the day with her. If you need a ride to the hospital after your classes, I'll pick you up."

"She seemed so sick, Dad. I've never seen her like that." Laura scrambled some eggs, put two pieces of bread in the toaster and poured some juice for both of them. Peter was surprised that Laura was being helpful. She usually complained if she had to do a minimum amount of work around the house.

"The doctors told her not to have any more plastic surgery, Laura. She chose to do this. I'm sorry she's suffering the consequences, but there's nothing we can do except wait for the antibiotic to work. I'm certain when we see her this afternoon she'll be better. Are you ready to leave? I'll drop you off at school."

"It's OK, Pop. Betsy's picking me up. She'll probably give me a ride to the hospital after school. It's on her way. Oops, here she is now. See you later. Bye." Laura picked up her backpack, gave Peter a quick kiss and ran out the door.

Peter sat down at the kitchen table and put his head in his hands. Could it get any worse? he wondered.

I must win that money. Making the team takes me one step closer to keeping the Mafia away.

Turner Academy
Monday Morning, May 11th

Ten o'clock found Laura and Betsy walking down the center hall of Turner Academy High School, heading for their English class. Laura was glum.

"Come on, Laura, your Mom will be fine. I know you're worried, but she is getting the best care," coaxed Betsy.

"It's not just my Mom. I've had it with Chad. He's selfish and thoughtless. I'm wasting my time with him…and he's really hurt me," sighed Laura.

Betsy put her arm around her friend. She felt sorry for Laura, but she was happy that Chad was out of Laura's life. Laura was a better person than he, and she should appreciate herself more.

Just then Chad and Chris appeared around the corner. "Hi, ladies." Chris smiled directly at Betsy, who smiled back.

Chad came forward and put his arm around Laura as usual. She backed away, saying loudly, "Never come near me or speak to me again."

"What's the matter with you?" he demanded.

"You are self-centered and thoughtless," she continued.

"Catch this one, Miss High and Mighty," he retorted.

"Leave me alone," said Laura as she stormed down the hall. She was shaking and did not want him to see her like that. The other three looked at her back as she hustled between other students hurrying to class.

"Come on, Betsy," said Chris taking her arm. "I'll walk you to class."

No one spoke to Chad who stood still, quietly fuming. No girl had ever spoken to him like that. Some nearby students who heard the exchange looked at Chad and seemed to be enjoying his discomfort. Chad turned and, head held high, left the school.

Laura felt awful. Her usual approach to life was to please everyone, but in the past few days, she began to realize this was not enough. Her feelings should be important, too. This fight with Chad was the first time she had stood up for herself, and she was scared. What if she had made a mistake? The day dragged on.

At dismissal she headed for the parking lot to meet Betsy who was giving her a ride to the hospital. Betsy waved at her as she approached and said, "I'm dropping off Chris, too. His house is on the way to the hospital ."

Just then they saw Chris running towards them. "Laura," smiled Chris. "Your friend, Betsy, is the best. She helped me all weekend with my economics project and when I handed it in today, guess what? Old Herman looked it over and told me to come back at the end of the day. Well, when I got there he was discussing the project with some other teachers and they all thought it was the best work they'd seen in years! I got an A+, excuse me, Betsy and I got an A+." With that he hugged Betsy and kissed her cheek.

Laura smiled. She was happy to see Betsy with a boy who was interested in her. It was about time. "Betsy, let's get going. I want to get to the hospital as soon as I can."

As they drove along, Chris and Betsy reviewed the project, and Laura sat quietly with her thoughts. As Betsy pulled into Chris's driveway he touched her shoulder from the backseat. "Thanks for the ride. I really appreciate it. I hope your mom is doing better, Laura. I'll call you later, Betsy."

Betsy told Laura that she thought Chris was great, and she hoped to see more of him. Laura gave her a weak smile, but said nothing. Her thoughts were elsewhere.

The Hospital
Monday, Late Afternoon, May 11th

Peter met Laura in the hospital cafeteria. "Have a good day sweetheart?"

" No, Dad, Mr. Montgomery gave us a pop quiz in history. I don't see why we need to know about World War II anyway. It's over and done with."

"We need to know about the past, Laura, so we won't make the same mistakes in the future. Let's grab a quick bite and then head up to the fourth floor."

Surprisingly the hospital food was good, and Laura munched on a turkey wrap. "How is Mom today?"

"Still the same, Laura. I saw Dr. Johnson late morning and if no progress is made by the time Dr. Williams makes rounds, she goes to Intensive Care. Look at that as a good thing, Laura. It's the best care in the hospital."

Gloria was in bed 4B, but fortunately she didn't have a roommate. She was still hooked up to all sorts of machines.

"Hi, Mom," said Laura as she kissed her mother. "I brought you some magazines--Vogue, Elle and Town and Country." Gloria nodded her head weakly. She seemed very lethargic. Just then Dr. Johnson's partner walked into the room. He was 36, sandy-haired and drop dead gorgeous, as Laura would later describe him to Betsy.

"Hello, I'm Dr. Williams. Are you Mr. Drummond?"

"Yes, please call me Peter. This is our daughter, Laura. How is my wife doing, Doctor?"

Dr. Williams had been flipping through Gloria's chart. He steered both of them into the hallway. As they moved through the door, Peter realized the doctor didn't want to talk in front of his wife.

"She keeps spiking a temperature although she hasn't been on the IV antibiotic for 24 hours yet. I'm actually very concerned about her condition. Not only is her temperature high, but she is becoming disoriented. I've decided to put her in Intensive Care. First, I'd like to ask you a few questions. She was very sick when she came in. Do you know anything about this clinic in Costa Rica?"

"Gloria had checked it out thoroughly. She contacted some Board called ISAS."

"Yes, it's the International Society of Aesthetic Surgery."

"Her surgeon met the compliance standards. I think she even had some friends who went there. I didn't see it so I don't know anything about it. It actually was called a "surgical vacation" where you had your plastic surgery and then could see the sights in the country. Do you think she got the infection there?"

"I honestly don't know, Peter. It bothers me that the patient called it a surgery vacation. You should be resting in a clinic or home and not out touring. The point is we have to get rid of the infection. Look, she's asleep now. I advise you to go home. She's been sleeping most of the day. It's the body's way of trying to cope. It will take awhile to get her settled in Intensive Care. The first time you could see her would be nine p.m. Hours are very limited."

"Laura, I'd love some bottled water. Would you go down to the gift shop and get one for me? I'll meet you downstairs by the front entrance. I have a few questions I'd like to ask Dr. Williams."

"Sure, Dad. I know you want me out of the way. See you Dr. Williams." Laura went back into the room and kissed her mother. She patted her dad's shoulder as she walked to the elevator.

Peter waited until she was out of earshot before asking, "Dr. Williams, if my wife is so sick that you are putting her in Intensive Care, what is the bottom line?"

"Peter, why don't you call me Ed. I want your wife to be monitored very closely. We're doing everything to kill the infection, but it has really taken hold."

"Thank you, Ed, I know you're taking good care of her. I'll be back tonight at nine."

The Drummond Home
Monday Evening, May 11th

Peter pulled the car into the garage. He didn't want to leave it outside for fear of another episode with a mob member. It had taken over a week to get the car repaired. Both got out and went into the house. "How does a cup of cocoa sound, Laura?"

"It sounds even better with marshmellows, Dad. I'm going to make a quick phone call and I'll meet you in the family room."

Peter opened the cupboard door and pulled out the cocoa and sugar, then grabbed the milk from the refrigerator. The kitchen was pristine. "No wonder," thought Peter. "We never eat together anymore. Gloria is always out at committee meetings, Laura's over at Betsy's and I've been spending too much time with Valerie."

Peter heated the cocoa and poured it into mugs, then floated marshmallows on top. Peter carried the mugs into the family room where Laura was curled up on the couch with her kitten, Mittens.

"Did you have a chance to make your phone call?"

"Yes, Dad, the person wasn't home. It wasn't important. Dad, I've never seen Mom look so awful. Is she going to be all right?" Laura looked like a little girl. She had pulled her hair back in a ponytail to scrub off her makeup and she appeared ten rather than seventeen.

"Her doctors are the best, Laura. Your mom's had infections before. Hopefully this one will clear up, too."

Peter took a good look at Laura. She had Mittens lying on her chest, and was stroking her fur. "I wonder if Gloria has given her the sex talk? I hope she has, otherwise it's long overdo.

I really don't know much about my own daughter. In escaping the mundane life of my marriage I also abandoned fatherhood. When Gloria gets out of the hospital we're going to be a family again. I'm going to insist she cut back on her volunteer work."

"Laura, time for homework. I'm going back to the hospital at nine. I'll also be seeing your mother during the day tomorrow, but visiting hours are very limited. Could you sit with her tomorrow night while I'm at the tournament meeting?"

"Dad, I'll be happy to sit with Mom tomorrow. Give her my love now."

Peter put his arms around Laura. "You're a good girl. When Mom gets home we're going to take a family vacation." Then he left to go back to the hospital.

The Hospital
Tuesday, Late Afternoon, May 12th

Laura went directly to the hospital from school. She kept thinking of how poorly her mom looked yesterday. Hopefully today, Gloria would be somewhat better.

Gloria and Laura were not close. Laura's mother always seemed busy with the problems of others which she answered with fundraisers. In addition, as she grew older, Gloria spent considerable time and money on her appearance. She seemed to fear losing her good looks.

Laura tried to please her parents while involving herself in a social life where she worked diligently to have her peers like her. She did not realize her friends were drawn to her because they recognized that she was basically a good person.

Peter greeted her as she entered Gloria's room, then left immediately for the golf clinic and tournament meeting. Gloria was dozing, and Laura was asked to wait in the lounge until the next visiting period.

The next visiting time was at dinner. The nurse woke Gloria. Laura was happy that her mother opened her eyes and smiled when she saw her daughter. Laura wanted to talk to her mom, but it was Gloria who, with difficulty, started the conversation. She seemed determined to speak to Laura even though her words came out in a whisper at times.

"Laura, it is so good to see you. I've been dreaming about you as a baby. You were so pretty and so good. I was a lucky mom."

Laura could feel herself choking up.

Gloria continued. "Now look at me! I worked all those years to please and help others and I neglected my own." She gazed at Laura. "Please forgive me."

Laura started to cry. "Mom, I love you and I admire your hard work."

"But I was never satisfied, Laura. I thought people liked me for what I could do for them. Then I got older and I saw my looks were starting to go. I foolishly felt that I would not be liked if I did not look good. So I started a regimen of nips, tucks, peels, lifts and botox, and here I am a mess."

"You'll be fine, Mom. This is a good hospital and your doctors are the best." Laura stroked Gloria's arm, trying not to disturb the tube inserted in her hand.

"Laura, learn from me. Appreciate yourself. Do not live for the approval of others. You are a very pretty girl. Don't sell yourself short, learn from my mistakes."

"Oh, Mom, you do not know how much I needed you to tell me this. I need you so to help me be the person I should be. Please get well soon and we will be together as a family."

Gloria smiled weakly. "I love you, Baby," she whispered.

Laura pulled herself together and tried to get her mother to eat, but it was hopeless. Gloria could not swallow more than a few bites. Then she fell back to sleep. The visiting period was over so Laura returned to the lounge to do her homework.

High Ridge Country Club
Tuesday, May 12th

Ted Rankin had a bucket of balls put by the practice green. He had decided a lesson in chipping would be the most valuable. Sunset Hills would be the first course they would be playing Saturday, May 23rd, and the greens were much faster than High Ridge's.

Hank was the first to show up. "Help yourself to some practice balls, Mr. Hawthorne. The other three should be here shortly."

The next to arrive was Brad and he started putting. Ted made the comment that Brad was not following through with his putter to the hole.

"Maybe that's why I three-putted three greens during qualifying. Thank God I was able to chip close enough on the other holes to one-putt."

Peter and Connie pulled up to the parking lot at the same time. As they got out of their cars Connie asked, "How's Gloria, Peter? Did Dr. Johnson help you?"

"Gloria's been hospitalized, Connie. They are optimistic and feel she should be fine after a course of antibiotics. Laura is sitting with her while I'm at this golf clinic and meeting." Peter did not want Connie to know Gloria was in Intensive Care and wonder why Peter was at the course and not at the hospital.

"Who is 'they,' Peter? I thought Dr. Johnson was treating her."

"Dr. Johnson has a new partner. He seems very well-informed. About your age, Connie. He actually is part of the foursome from Sunset Hills. I think he qualified in first position."

"I knew Ben was looking for a partner. I guess I'm out of the loop. He must have excellent credentials if Ben took him in."

"I think he trained at the University of Michigan. From what I understand his father became ill and the son came back to New York to practice so he could be near his father and oversee his care."

By this time they had reached the locker rooms. Both disappeared to put on their golf shoes and proceed to the practice green.

Ted gathered the four of them at the edge of the practice area. "OK, congratulations," Ted remarked. " You probably need this practice session less than anyone, but I thought this might be a time to discuss strategy. My thought is that you play a conservative game unless you've fallen way behind and then go for every shot."

"That sounds reasonable," replied Connie. "Let them make the mistakes." Both Peter and Brad nodded their heads in agreement.

"I don't know, Ted," said Hank. "That's not my style. I have to go all out. I have to let 'the big dog eat' when I hit my driver. If I think I can make a par five hole in two I'll hit my fairway wood even if it's a low percentage shot. Ya'll go ahead and play safe and I'll make the birdies. If you're not the 'lead dog' the view never changes."

"I guess everyone will just have to play their own game," Connie said. "Now impart some wisdom on the greenside shots."

Ted gave a short lesson, and then the five of them decided to have dinner at the club. Peter tried to reach Laura on her cell phone, but realized it probably did not work in the hospital.

About 7:45 p.m. the group adjourned to the President's room where Jim was setting up for the meeting. The mahogany paneling gave a rich glow to the room. Vases filled with roses and baby's breath were placed throughout. The mantle of the fireplace held trophies dating back to 1930. And the "Piece de Resistance" was the glass bowl with $250,000 in cash sitting at the front of the room. Of course, two Safety Assured guards were flanking the money.

Just then the club receptionist came up to Peter Drummond and handed him a note. Peter opened it and saw it was a message from Dr. Johnson. It asked him to come to the hospital immediately. Peter did not bother to say goodbye, but hurried out the door.

"I wonder what that was all about," said Brad. "The meeting's about to begin."

Putting for the Green

"Peter's wife is in the hospital, Brad," Connie said. "I hope she hasn't taken a turn for the worse."

Groups of four representing the other three clubs started to drift in and take seats around the room. Jim had set up a bar with a bartender. Coffee and tea were also offered. The famous High Ridge chocolate chip cookies were mounded on a platter and disappearing quickly.

At seven o'clock Jim started the meeting. "I'd like to welcome the members from Sunset Hills, Turtle Creek and Hudson View along with our own foursome from High Ridge. I thought we might begin by each club introducing its members."

Introductions went around the room. Connie noticed that she was the only woman participating. When she heard the name, Ed Williams, she realized he was Ben's new partner. He was one gorgeous man, she thought. Little did she know that Ed was also looking her over, and liking what he saw. "I can't believe Ben hasn't had us meet," he thought.

"Now that the introductions are over, I'd like to discuss the ground rules. Our first match will take place at Sunset Hills, then Hudson View, Turtle Creek and ending at High Ridge. Each player qualified in a certain position one through four. All number one positions will play each other, number two positions and so on.

On May 23rd the High Ridge team will play Turtle Creek and Sunset Hills will play Hudson View. One point will be awarded for the front nine, one for the back and one point for overall for a total of three points. If there is a tie each contestant receives one half a point. At the end of the three tournament days the team with the most combined points wins the million dollars. Of course, each club will have a chance to display the cash. This will happen on the day the tournament is played at that particular club. Any questions?"

"Yes," Hank said. "Are there any more chocolate chip cookies?" There was much laughter and nodding of heads. As the meeting broke up members from each club started to mingle near the bar. Golf stories were traded and competitors sized up. Ed Williams made his way over to Connie.

"Why has Ben been hiding you?" Ed asked. "I know you're his protegee. Actually, Connie, we just used your partner for a cardiology consult on Gloria Drummond. She's having an irregular heartbeat. I'm glad she's being monitored in Intensive Care."

"I'm on call tomorrow, so I'll be seeing her. Peter never said she was sick enough to be in Intensive Care."

"You know that family members sometimes diminish the severity of the problem because they can't think a loved one might be in difficulty. Let's switch the topic. Can you find a day where I might take you to dinner. Are you free Saturday night?"

"Aren't you being a little presumptuous? You're just assuming I want to go out with you."

"How about if I sweeten the pot. I'll ask Ben to go with us."

"You know the way to a woman's heart. OK, if Ben can go, then I'll go, too."

The Hospital
Tuesday Evening, May 12th

About seven-thirty, Gloria began to gasp and thrash around. By the time Peter arrived, Gloria had been sedated and lay still. Laura was nodding off in the waiting room. As Peter approached Laura, he saw Dr. Johnson by Gloria's door.

Dr. Johnson looked grave as he said, "It doesn't look good, Peter. If you have any special words for Gloria, now is the time. The infection is running rampant through her body."

Peter entered Gloria's room and Dr. Johnson brought Laura in from the waiting area. The two of them sat, one on each side of the bed. Only the beeping of the machines made any sound. They waited silently and prayed.

Then Gloria's breathing became loud and hoarse. Laura ran to the nurse's station. When she returned, Gloria's eyes were open and Peter was holding her hand. Gloria gasped, "No matter what I did, you were the love of my life. Please take care of Laura for me."

Laura moved to the other side of the bed, tears streaming down her face. "Stay with us, Mom. We need you."

Gloria convulsed, coughing. Finally she lay back. "I did what I thought was best. I always loved you both. Forgive me if I neglected you."

Then Dr. Johnson asked Peter and Laura to step outside. A few minutes later he joined them. "She won't last the night, I'm sorry. Stay with her. It will help her. Do you want a member of the clergy to come?"

Peter nodded as Laura started crying uncontrollably. The two of them went in to say goodbye.

Battery Park City
Late Tuesday Night, May 12th

Big Carmine sat behind the wheel of his Lincoln Navigator on a dark street near the south end of the West Side Highway. A large box of cookies sat on the seat beside him. Pignolis were his favorite and since he had to meet Don Sericusa near Little Italy, a side trip to Ferrara's for the best pignolis in town was a necessity.

Carmine was munching his tenth pignoli when the heavy black Mercedes pulled up in front of him. He exited the SUV, dusting the crumbs from his lips.

The driver motioned Carmine into the backseat. Carmine squeezed himself into the car and found Vito Sericusa seated to his right. The Don was an immaculately dressed, slightly built seventy-year-old. He was well-recognized as a highly intelligent and diligent listener.

After preliminary small talk about business, Don Sericusa asked Carmine about the reason for this meeting. Carmine handed him the clipping, Close Up With Colette, from Saturday's Westchester Weekly. The Don dismissed Carmine, warning him to keep silent about this opportunity. He promised that he would contact Carmine in the near future.

Vito Sericusa began his professional life at the age of 12 as a petty thief on Bay 13th Street in Brooklyn. His quick mind, ability to sense weakness in others and astute business sense attracted the attention of well-placed mob members. Vito was a "made man" by his twenty-fifth birthday.

As the years passed, less and less was seen of Vito in public, but within the Family his power grew. By the time he was fifty, he controlled the New York West Side from the Battery to Yonkers. By age sixty, Westchester and Duchess counties were under his control. No business in his territory escaped The Don's scrutiny.

Don Vito's Home
Wednesday Afternoon, May 12th

Vito Sericusa's home was an historic colonial in an upscale area of Pelham. He had been behind his desk for hours--thinking and planning. Grabbing one million dollars that is sitting out in the open sounded difficult, but it could be done. Success lay in the details.

Where in the High Ridge Country Club was the money to be displayed? Who would do the job? How would they gain access to the building? How protected was the money? Guards? Electronic surveillance? How would the boys get away? Lots of questions. Now to find the answers.

Vito had resources. He had men and he had connections, but no connections in the High Ridge Country Club. Someone would have to case the place to find out what he needed to know. He had another very useful resource, an extensive laundry and dry cleaning business that he used to launder money--how ironic.

This business allowed him ready access to company uniforms. His guys could pass themselves off as a variety of workers who would be readily admitted anywhere.

Vito placed a call to the High Ridge Country Club. The conversation went like this. "Hello, I'm supposed to play golf with some friends at your club next week. They asked me to pick a day. They mentioned that you're closed one day a week. I can't remember what day that is. What day is it that you are closed?...Mondays? You're closed on Monday? Well, I guess I won't pick that day to play. Thank you for your help. See you soon."

Vito smiled and said to himself, "That was easy." Now he could put his plan together.

Romano Funeral Parlor
Thursday, Mid-Afternoon, May 14th

Babs was tired of hanging around the funeral home. Gloria looked so wooden even though the director had done an impeccable job with Gloria's hair and makeup. "I don't know why they have open coffins anyway," she thought. Terribly morbid.

She noticed that Hank had gone outside for a breath of fresh air. Quietly she slipped out, too, and found Hank lounging against the fence surrounding the funeral home. "Hey, I'd ask you for a cigarette if I smoked," said Babs. She leaned against a pole next to Hank.

"If you smoked you'd probably end up inside like Gloria instead of out here flirting with me."

"You have an awfully high opinion of yourself, don't you, Hank. Where's Sarah by the way?"

"She's in her studio, as usual. She said she'd drop by later. Why are you out here, Babs? It's not for a suntan." Hank turned and caressed her arm.

"Careful, there are all sorts of people we know passing by. I wanted to talk to you about the golf tournament, specifically are you replacing Peter with Chip? He qualified in fifth place."

"The body's not quite cold yet, Babs. You want to discuss this now? What if Peter is still planning to play? A lot of money is at stake."

"All the more reason you should be replacing him with Chip. How can Peter play his best right now after this happened? He needs to be with his daughter." Babs leaned in and touched Hank's shoulder.

"Who should be careful now? We could find a more comfortable place to finish our conversation."

"I'm certain we've already been missed. Think about this seriously, Hank. Don't you want what's best for the team?"

"I'm curious to know why the push to oust Peter? That money look awfully good to you? A few trips to Atlantic City? I'm not saying I disagree with you, Babs. Do you want to do a little persuading?"

"Of course I'd like to see Chip on the team. The money does look good, Hank. I think we'd better go back inside. I'll go first."

As Babs started to leave, Hank grabbed her hand firmly. "I want you, Babs. I've never wanted anything so much."

Millie and Brad were walking up the steps and saw the scenario. "How inappropriate," whispered Millie.

"None of our business," Brad replied.

"Just like a man," Millie said as she reached the top step. "And I don't mean Hank." Brad opened the door and they walked inside.

Babs and Hank started to walk up the steps. "Millie sure gave us a dirty look, Hank."

"Do you care what that fat cow thinks?"

"Millie has a good heart, Hank. And I like to look at her as pleasingly plump. We need to be careful though."

"Does that mean there's some hope for me?"

"You just like the thrill of the chase. You wouldn't know what to do with me if you caught me. I can run fast, but I sure could slow down if Chip gets on the team." Babs turned to Hank and winked.

"I'm going in first, Hank. Wait a couple of minutes and then come inside." Babs put on her somber face as she walked in the door.

The first person Babs ran into was Millie. "Hi, Millie, I know you saw Hank and me outside, and I'd like to explain."

Millie, in her forthright way replied, "It did look a little odd, Babs, Hank holding your hand at a wake for one of your best friends."

"Actually, Millie, Hank was trying to stop me from going inside and giving Peter a piece of my mind. He's still playing on the team which I think is disrespectful of Gloria. What does Brad think?"

"Whatever Brad thinks is none of my business. There is a week and a half before final decisions have to be made. Who knows if Peter will be playing or not. Why don't you come with me, and we'll see if we can comfort Laura." Millie linked arms with Babs and basically dragged her over to the corner where Laura was sitting alone.

Chip walked into the funeral home as the hours for the wake were ending. He looked smart in a Ralph Lauren blue suit with a Hermes tie. He had a very successful law practice and became a workaholic after no children arrived in his life.

He walked up to Peter and put his arm around him. "Sorry I'm so late, Peter. I got stuck in court and just got out. Are you holding up alright, old man?"

"Thanks, Chip. I'm coping. It's funny, I was just thinking about when we were in law school and you introduced me to Gloria. She was the roommate of the girl you were dating at the time. It was spring and the four of us would ride around in your convertible with the top down."

"Yes, unfortunately Gloria's roommate found someone with a bigger and better car."

"Yeah, Chip, but you would've ended up in Iowa where Ellie's parents were from. I remember she was pressuring you. This way we got to remain good friends. Plus you sure have a looker now in Babs. Listen, Chip, could we go into the other room and talk. I really need your advice. Let me see if Millie will take care of Laura getting to dinner."

"Sure, Peter. Would you like to grab a bite to eat at the diner across the way?"

"Thanks, Chip, but Connie has invited us for dinner before tonight's visitation. I just need a few minutes."

Peter and Chip walked over to Millie and Babs. Babs gave Chip a hug and said she would see him at home. Millie was going to drop Laura, Gloria's brother and wife at Connie's for dinner. After a short conversation the men walked to a little alcove off the main room.

"Peter, whatever I can do to help, I will. What do you need?"

"First, if Laura doesn't object I'd still like to play in the money tournament. I'm only telling you that I desperately need the cash. I've gotten myself into a bad situation. I wondered what you and the others would think? I know you would be the one to take my place if I dropped out."

"Peter, if you need the money then go for it. There's nothing more you can do for Gloria. There are plenty of women to mother Laura, but if I were you I would have a 'heart to heart' with her. Treat her like an adult. Explain why you need to play. I've never had children, but I think being honest with anyone works the best. Peter, If you're doing this for the money, could I loan it to you?"

"No. I appreciate your generosity, Chip, but I have to handle this money problem myself. Which brings me to the next question. I know I haven't practiced law for many years, but I'd like to get back into it. Would there be any job for me, no matter how lowly, in your firm?"

Chip thought for a minute. "Peter, I can find you a place in the real estate part of our firm, and then later switch you over to litigation. Come and talk to me after the tournament's over and hopefully High Ridge has won the money."

Nelson Home
Thursday, May 14th

Chip arrived home and found Babs whipping up some spaghetti putanesca. She poured him a glass of Chianti, and he took off his jacket and tie before sitting down on the stool at the breakfast bar.

Babs had just remodeled the kitchen, and it was state of the art, from the six burner gas stove, and Sub Zero refrigerator to the imported Italian tile backsplash. Babs was an excellent cook with Italian food her specialty. She worked as a waitress in an Italian restaurant at one time and picked up many recipes.

She worked her way up to assistant chef, and when Chip wanted a small dinner party at the restaurant, the head chef sent her to deal with Chip. It was love at first sight for Chip, and Babs decided this was an adorable meal ticket. They were married six months later. Chip had kept his boyish good looks, but thanks to Babs, his middle had expanded.

"What did Peter want to talk about, Chip?" asked Babs. She tossed the salad, put it on plates, and shaved some Parmesan cheese over both.

"He actually asked me for a job," replied Chip, not mentioning Peter's money problem. "I think I can find a place for him in the firm."

Babs sat down next to Chip, putting his salad plate before him. "Wasn't that wake horrible? I hate funerals. Do you think we have to go back tonight?"

"Yes, Babs, you were one of Gloria's best friends. We have to show support for Peter and Laura. By the way, you need to watch yourself with Hank. I heard some rumors you two were getting cozy. Of course I denied them, but I don't expect to hear anything else."

"Hank and I just like to kid around, Chip. People can be mean gossips. We were just discussing that Peter should drop out of the tournament and you would take his place."

"Peter isn't quitting, Babs. He asked my opinion and I told him he should remain on the team. It will do him good."

Chip approached Babs from behind as she was stirring the sauce. He took her gently by the shoulders and kissed her neck. "You know, Babs, I think sometimes you get a little bored. I have some extra money to play around with. You used to talk about opening your own restaurant. If you still would like to do it, we could go looking at places."

Chip sat down started to dig into his pasta. "The dinner looks great, Babs. Mario Molto has nothing on you. Thanks."

When they had finished eating Chip announced, "I have some work to do before we go back to the funeral home." He picked up his dishes and put them into the sink. He went into his study and closed the door.

Babs started putting the dishes in the dishwasher. "I guess I'd better start being more careful," she thought. "I wonder who was talking to Chip? I do have a good life with him, and the bottom line is that I love being his wife. He's right about my being bored. I haven't thought about the restaurant idea in ages."

"Maybe this would be the perfect project for me. Now that Gloria's dead, I won't have all those fund raisers. I wonder if Ann would be my interior designer? Maybe I could get Sarah to do some murals." Babs snapped the dishwasher shut and grinned as she left the room.

High Ridge Country Club
Monday Midday, May 18th

The High Ridge Country Club sat atop a hill overlooking the golf course. It was set at the end of a circular drive about a quarter mile from the road.

The main building dated back over one hundred and fifty years. Originally, it was the home of a wealthy farmer. Its dark grey slate roof and gabled windows could be seen above the building. The exterior was white with black shutters and trim. The enclosed entrance portico was flanked by large marble urns containing seasonal plantings. The six steps at the entrance led to a handsome wrought iron and wood outer door. The portico was twelve feet square and the inner door was made of polished oak and leaded stained glass.

Beyond this door was a very large foyer, at least sixty feet square. The walls were light in color with dark wood molding. Two twenty foot oil paintings of nineteenth century golf scenes were hung on the walls at each side of the entrance. Oil paintings of pastoral scenes and a tapestry covered the other walls. Two well-upholstered sofas, four club chairs and occasional tables were placed along the walls. The most noticeable aspect of the entrance foyer, however, was the large ebony carved pedestal in its exact center. This six foot piece was circled by a four foot deep green tufted and fringed velvet bench. The pedestal supported a large antique urn containing fresh flowers that rose another two to three feet toward the impressive tray ceiling twenty feet away.

Opposite the entrance was a large enclosed porch that looked on to the summer outdoor dining veranda and beyond it to a swimming pool. Hallways from this porch led to the bar, kitchen and dining room to the left and to restrooms and the banquet hall to the right. The pro shop and locker rooms were beyond and somewhat below the dining room due to the elevation of the ground.

An arched recess thirty feet along the wall on the left housed the receptionist's work area which included a very valuable Chippendale desk complete with chair and a computer work station hidden behind an intricately decorated screen.

Angelo DeAngelo and Nunzio stopped their white van in the circular driveway at the front of High Ridge Country Club. Both men were wearing green jackets with the logo for Nancy's Flower Shop decorating the breast pocket.

Angelo entered the foyer and headed for the reception area. "Hi dere, lovely lady. Can you tell me where one ninety four Ridge Lane is located? We have a large order of flowers to deliver before noon."

The receptionist looked up to see a man with lively blue eyes and dark curly hair. His quick smile and sincere manner certainly got her attention.

"I'm sorry," she said, "but you are very lost. The street outside is Ridge Road not Ridge Lane. Ridge Lane is in the next town about five miles away."

At this point Nunzio entered talking loudly on his cell phone. "Yeah, we are lost, but now we are gettin' directions. Yeah, yeah we'll get dere on time." He ended the call and then addressed the receptionist. "Lady, I need the can."

"It's the second door on the right when you enter the hallway off the porch." She pointed to the porch as she spoke.

"Please excuse my driver," said Angelo. "His manners are terrible. We are embarrassed to let him out of the truck," he quipped.

She laughed at his comment and then gave him directions to their destination.

Angelo listened attentively to the list of turns and stop signs. When she was finished, he thanked her and asked, "Where is everyone? Dis is a huge place and you're all alone. What gives?"

She smiled and explained that the Club was officially closed on Mondays. She, three administrative staff upstairs in the offices, and the maintenance staff were the only ones around.

"Des is some big room," he said looking around the foyer. He pointed at the pedestal. "Dat's some large flower stand."

"Well," she replied, "on the last Sunday in May it's going to support one million dollars in cash. That's the prize for the golf tournament."

"You gotta be kiddin," he exclaimed. "One million dollars. Dis is some classy place."

"What's out there?" he asked walking towards the porch. She followed him, chattering away about the distinctive architectural features of the building and its history. She was happy to have such a cute guy for company on this quiet day. She did what she could to delay his departure.

"Would you like a drink?" she asked, heading toward the bar. "I mean a soft drink. I know you are working."

"Dat would be great," he replied. He followed her into the bar and accepted a cola.

Nunzio now returned, talking on his cell again. "I'm telling ya, Philomina, I'll be home on time tonight. Yes, I'll bring the veal cutlets from Mauro's for dinner." He hung up. "That woman makes me crazy. What are you doin'? Partyin'? We got flowers to deliver. It's already eleven-thirty. I hope you got directions.".

Angelo gave his glass to the receptionist and headed for the front door. "You have a nice place here. Enjoy." He closed the door after him.

The two entered the van and sped down the driveway, laughing. When they found a pull in about a mile away, Nunzio stopped the van and took out his cell phone. Everything they needed was on the picture phone. On the phone was a video of the foyer, the pedestal, the hallways, bar, porch and bathroom of the High Ridge Country Club. They had done their job well. Don Sericusa will be happy with them.

Don Vito's Home
Wednesday, May 20th

Don Sericusa sat at his desk gazing at the man seated before him. His thoughtful facial expression encouraged this visitor to give specific details and draw conclusions about the information he was presenting.

The Don recognized that while the speech and manners of the young man were not polished, the fellow possessed a sharp intellect. In addition, Angelo had a definite capacity to make analogies and foresee problems that could arise. He even made suggestions on how to solve these problems. The more the Don heard, the more he was impressed by Angelo DeAngelo.

If Angelo got rid of his Brooklyn accent and dressed more appropriately, he could be easily accepted in the best society. More importantly, he could move up in the Family. The Don made a mental note to have someone work on Angelo's image when this job was over.

When Angelo finished his presentation, the two men again viewed the video taken by Nunzio on his cell. Angelo explained, step by step, how the money could be stolen. The Don liked his ideas and added a few touches of his own. The meeting ended with the Don telling Angelo that he would be the one to bring the money to him after the heist. Angelo was to be the boss of the job, but he was not to enter the building.

Neopolitan Club
Thursday, May 21st

Angelo developed his plan and thought about the team he would use for the heist. He needed someone familiar with electrical circuits, surveillance cameras and plumbing. That security camera on the foyer ceiling pointing at the pedestal had to be controlled.

A plumbing problem would cause a diversion and allow a stranger to enter the premises while the guards were on duty. He needed someone who could do both jobs and be non-threatening to the country club's management. He asked the Don for a recommendation. Vito was pleased that this young guy was smart enough to understand his limitations and even smarter to ask the Don for his advice. Angelo continued to rise in Don Vito's esteem.

The Don stated that landscape sprinkler maintenance required skill in electronics and plumbing. The Club management would not be suspicious of someone from the company they used for watering the grounds and the golf course. Vito used his laundry business to supply Angelo with uniforms from Logrosso and Sons Plumbing and Sprinkler Maintenance. This is the company that services the watering system for High Ridge Country Club.

The Don also recommended a mechanic from a local garage to handle the electronic and plumbing part of the job. This man was multi-talented. In addition to his technical skills, he was also a local drug pusher and long time member of Don Sericusa's mob. His nickname, Gap Tooth, spoke volumes about his appearance.

In order to accomplish his assigned task, Gap Tooth would have to disguise his appearance.

Nunzio, long recognized as a top notch wheel man, was to serve as the driver and perform any other tasks that might be needed.

So Angelo had a plan and a team. Now he had to carry out the task.

Sunset Hills
Saturday, May 23rd

Connie walked off the eighteenth green after shaking her opponent's hand. He had declined the offer of a drink as his family was celebrating his daughter's birthday and he did not want to be late.

Winning two out of three points thrilled Connie. She was even through eight holes, but her opponent managed to birdie the ninth so she lost the front nine. High Ridge was playing Turtle Creek today, and Sunset Hills was taking on Hudson View.

Standing before the scoreboard to record her score, she saw that Hank, playing in first position, had lost two points to his opponent, and Peter had won all three of his points. She turned to see if Brad had finished, as he was playing behind her. "Broke even," Brad said as he came up beside Connie.

That meant that High Ridge had garnered seven and a half points out of twelve. Turtle Creek followed with four and a half, Hudson View, three, and Sunset Hills in first place with nine.

Connie looked around to see if Ed Williams was still there. Then she remembered Ben was covering for him until he finished. He must be at the hospital by now.

Her date last Saturday night had been wonderful. Ben, a great buffer, had said flattering things about both of them. Connie felt an instant attraction, but nothing much had happened. Ed and she seemed to be playing telephone tag all week.

As Connie walked into the pro shop she noticed the huge crowd around the Waterford bowl. It now contained $250,000 from Sunset Hills added to the same amount from High Ridge for a total of $500,000. "I hope those guards never have to use their guns," Connie mused.

Then she ran into Hank. "Of course Sunset Hills would get nine points. It's their home course," whined Hank. "It was like putting on a billiard table."

Connie wanted to tell Hank to suck it up, but instead she said, "Don't be discouraged, Hank. We'll have our chance when we play Sunset Hills at our course. Meanwhile, we're only one and a half behind." Hope that sounded like a team player, Connie thought. "See you at Hudson View tomorrow."

As Connie walked to her car, her cell phone rang. "Dr. Carson," she answered. "Oh, hi, Ed. Congratulations on getting three points. Yes, I managed two. Putting was my nemesis at your course. I'd love to go out tomorrow night. Good luck with your match tomorrow."

Connie hung up and broke into a big smile. She picked her clubs up at the bag drop and for once didn't think about cardiology.

Hudson View
Sunday, May 24th

Hudson View was the hilliest of the four courses, and Hank was panting by the time he walked up the huge slope to the eighteenth green. He was worn out due to a sexual night with Sarah. She can be one hot tomato under the covers, he thought. The housekeeper had made an excellent dinner, and Sarah and he polished off almost two bottles of Chateauneuf du Pape.

She certainly was a trophy wife. Why do I fool around when I have so much at home? Sarah had admitted that her profession had become too consuming, and she would try to make more time for Hank.

What she didn't tell him was that Millie had had a frank talk with her. Millie had pointed out that if Sarah wanted to keep her husband she better be more available. Sarah was even coming here this afternoon to see how he did. They were going to grab a quick bite afterward.

Hank decided he had better concentrate on this last putt. His opponent had bogeyed so with this five foot putt for a par he would finish the back nine one up. This would give him three points and a much better feeling than yesterday. The putt broke from left to right, probably one ball out. Hank changed his mind at the last minute and decided to play it left side but in the hole. He drained it! As Hank looked up he saw Sarah watching from the sidelines. She smiled and pantomimed a clap.

Hank walked off the green and gave Sarah a hug. Then he turned around to wait for his teammates. Quite a number of High Ridge members had come out not only to cheer them on, but to see the

Putting for the Green

$750,000 pot. Safety Assured had stationed two additional guards at the driveway entrance to the club, and only members of the four clubs were allowed through.

"Not so good," said Peter dejectedly. "Only one point."

Connie was next and held up two fingers. Brad broke even with one and a half points. As they looked at the board, High Ridge and Sunset Hills were tied with fifteen points apiece, Turtle Creek was next with ten and a half and Hudson View finished with seven and a half.

Connie, Peter, Hank and Sarah decided to go in and have a drink. Brad needed to pick up Millie and the four kids as they had tickets to the circus.

A bottle of champagne was ordered and they took their glasses to stand in front of the money. "I can't believe that's what $750,000 in cash looks like," marveled Connie.

"I hope there are no incidents," Peter said. "Two guards in here don't seem like a lot."

Just then Ed Williams walked up to Connie. "Hey, no fraternizing with the enemy," joked Hank.

"Great tournament so far," said Ed. "It will be a suspenseful match next week since we're tied. I'm going to take this young lady away and see if I can get some trade secrets from her."

Sarah suddenly spoke up. "Hi, I'm Sarah Hawthorne. Hank and I are going to have a bit of dinner. Would you like to join us?" She looked at Connie. "Maybe Hank and you could give us a blow by blow of what happened today."

Ed said, "You sure have the lingo down pat. Nothing makes a golfer happier than going over a tournament hole by hole. What kind of food are you interested in? Connie and I had talked about having Chinese tonight."

Hank seemed extremely pleased that Sarah had wanted to go out with Ed and Connie. "Chinese sounds good to me. What about you, Sarah?"

"Chinese it is. Just let me call Betsy and see if everything is OK at home. She's babysitting. I told them to order a pizza for dinner. I think Laura is there, also. By the way, since Laura is at our house, would you like to go, too, Peter?"

"That's a nice thought, Sarah, but I'm not much company these days. I really just want to go home and chill out." With that, Peter turned and left.

"Poor guy, it must be awful to go home to a lonely house," said Ed.

"I think that house was lonely before all this happened," replied Hank. "Sarah, call the girls so we can get going."

Sarah took out her cell phone and made the call. The pizza was on its way, and the girls were fine. Hank inquired about Chad and learned he was with Chris.

They agreed to meet at a popular Chinese restaurant near High Ridge. Ed held the door open to his Lexus. "It was nice of you to pick me up and take me to the tournament, Ed," Connie said as she slid into the beige leather seat.

Connie knew that Ed came from money. Both his parents had been doctors and owned several nursing homes in the area. Ed had been born twelve years after they were married, a pleasant surprise.

She thought it was wonderful that Ed had returned home after his father fell ill to help out. She knew Ed had wanted to stay at the University of Michigan to do research. Ben had filled her in on this information after he found out Connie and Ed were dating. "At least I hope we're dating," thought Connie. "I am attracted to this man."

Ed and Connie chatted about the tournament until they reached the restaurant. Hank and Sarah were already seated with little bottles of sake before them. "Guess my Jag beat your Lexus," joked Hank.

Connie inwardly groaned. "I only did this for Sarah, and now we're going to be subjected to Hank's bravado. I really wanted to get to know Ed better and instead I'm going to have to listen to Hank all night."

Ed ordered a Tsingtao beer and Connie had jasmine tea. Sarah put a stop to Hank's shenanigans by asking Ed to tell them all about himself as he was "the new kid on the block" so to speak.

It actually turned out to be a pleasant evening, and they were surprised when the pistachio ice cream and fortune cookies were brought. Ed broke his open and laughed when he read his fortune. He handed it to Connie and said, "I hope this comes true."

"A new joy will happen for a lifetime," she read out loud.

"Ah," said Hank. "You get him so lovestruck, Connie, he won't be able to concentrate when he plays me next week."

"Time to go," said Connie and they all headed for the parking lot.

"What a blowhard," said Ed as they got back into the car. "Sarah seems much too nice for him. I recognized her name from art circles. I've been perusing different galleries to find some paintings for my new home, and quite often her portraits turn up. Her style doesn't fit with my scheme, but I see she is branching out to do other work."

"Sarah is a sweetheart," said Connie. "I don't know what she sees in Hank, but something's there."

"Did you notice how protective he was of her? I think she likes that part of him. I got the impression she was abandoned as a child."

"Yes, both her parents were in a car accident and died when she was small. A grandmother raised her for awhile, but then she was shunted back and forth between other family members."

"She needs the stability that Hank gives her, and you can feel the sexual tension between them. I think that's a great part of their marriage. Sarah probably craves the love she lost as a child," Ed mused.

"You sound more like a psychiatrist then an internist, Ed," joked Connie. "Are you hanging out a different shingle?"

Just then Ed pulled up to Connie's townhouse. "How about if I come up and see your etchings?"

"That's a very old line, Ed. Try again."

"How about this, Connie?" Ed reached across the gearshift and took Connie in his arms, seeking her mouth with his. She lost herself in his soft, but persistent kiss, as he pulled her closer. "This is very uncomfortable, Connie. Can we go inside?"

"Ed this seems to be going rather fast. Can I trust you to put the skids on if we do go inside?"

"I'll follow your lead, Connie, but I must admit you're a very desirable woman."

Connie took out her key and opened the door. She threw her purse on the hall table and went into the kitchen to make some coffee. Her answering machine was blinking. As she played the messages Ed came up behind her and started massaging her neck. Then his hands drifted down to her waist.

"Looking forward to seeing you for our Memorial Day picnic," a male voice said on the recorder.

Ed turned her around, searching her face. "Do I have some competition, Connie?"

"If you consider a brother, competition, but actually he has some Giants coming to his barbecue tomorrow. That could prove interesting."

"Could I wangle an invitation, too?" asked Ed. "It seems like you're going to need some protection." He took her in his arms and gave her a kiss that started her heart pounding. He started to force his tongue into her mouth, and his right hand roamed over her body.

Connie pulled back and took a deep breath. "Ed, I don't know if I'm ready for this yet. I'm very attracted to you, but I'm not sure if this is the time to end up in bed."

Ed took her by the hand and led her over to the living room couch. "Let's just do some old-fashioned necking. I'm really excited about you, and just want to be close."

The next thirty minutes were exquisite as they slowly kissed and nuzzled each other. Ed laid soft kisses all over her face and neck. Connie took Ed's hand and put it over her breast. For a petite woman she was well endowed. Ed unbuttoned the top two buttons of her golf shirt and slid his hand inside, feeling her erect nipple.

I feel like a teenager in heat, Connie thought. Just then Ed stood up. Connie noticed the large bulge in his pants. "If we go any further I won't be able to stop, Connie. To be continued." He turned and walked out the door.

Connie didn't know what to think. It was too abrupt an ending and didn't leave her happy. She went into the bedroom and took off her clothes. She decided to take a nice leisurely bath to see if she could calm down. She turned on the jets and added some lavender bath salts. As she slid into the tub her breast was still tingling from Ed's touch.

High Ridge
Thursday, May 29th

Gap Tooth pulled into High Ridge Country Club and parked between two SUV's. His beige jumpsuit bore a logo that said Logrosso and Sons Plumbing and Sprinkler Maintenance.

He affixed a hairpiece and inserted his removable bridgework. Both disguises felt uncomfortable, and Gap Tooth might not have worn them except for the Don's insistence. He stood by the side view mirror and admitted, with a plumber's cap on he looked different. He opened the trunk of the car and removed his toolbox.

He sauntered into the building and approached the receptionist's desk at the High Ridge Country Club. "My boss sent me over to double check the sprinkler system. He knows you have a big tournament here on Sunday, and he wants the course to be perfectly watered."

"You're not kidding, we have a very special game on Sunday…a million dollar game," grinned the receptionist.

"Really sounds like golf is a rich man's game," Gap Tooth grinned back.

"I haven't seen you here before, so I'd better take you to the sprinkler system control box. It's right next to the electrical supply area."

"That's good," Gap Tooth replied. "The sprinkler system is powered by electricity. Nice to have them close together."

She lead him down a flight of stairs next to the restrooms and into a twelve foot square room that opened into another room to the right. "I'm sure you'll know what switches and things belong to the sprinkler system. I have to get back to my desk."

When she left, Gap Tooth made a thorough inspection of the room. Not only did it contain sprinkler system controls, but it also housed the central connections for the Club's water supply. He was even more impressed when he entered the adjoining room. Here was the main source of electricity for the clubhouse and the grounds including the golf course. Spread along one wall he saw the alarm system including the monitors for the remote cameras inside and outside the building.

Gap Tooth smiled, he was in command central for controlling all of High Ridge Country Club. After closing the door at the top of the stairs to insure warning of someone approaching, Gap Tooth began his work on the alarm system. He approached the monitor that focused on the pedestal in the foyer. This was the future resting place of the one million. On the day of the tournament, he would place a loop of tape into the monitor showing the money sitting on the pedestal.

Regardless of what action took place around the money, the only picture the monitor would show would be the view of the undisturbed pedestal. He would need to stop the camera recording for a few seconds to insert the loop of tape. There was little chance of anyone noticing that the tiny red light from the camera's lens had gone out for five or six seconds.

Next he approached the central alarm system that monitored the doors and windows. This system was old and temperamental. The portion for the pro shop was in the worst condition. Gap Tooth thought he could encourage it to break down on the day of the tournament. The wires from the area were pretty corroded. A few drops of acid on those terminals would end their job completely.

So much for the alarm system, now he had to assure that he would be at High Ridge the day of the tournament. Angelo had told him there would be a big wedding in the banquet area the Saturday afternoon before the tournament. "Close Up With Collette" reported that story in the Westchester Weekly, and Angelo's wife showed him the story last weekend. She should work for Don Vito, Gap Tooth thought. Nothing goes on in the gossip column that is missed by Rosie DeAngelo.

Gap Tooth knew that one area everyone would use during the wedding reception was the restrooms. A leak in there would have the Logrosso Plumbing and Sprinkler Maintenance Company summoned immediately. Gap Tooth would be sure to be at High Ridge on Saturday afternoon so that he could handle the problem. No call would have to be made to Carlo Logrosso who had no idea that his company's name was being used for the heist.

One way to assure that a leak would occur and not appear to be the result of tampering would be to have the sink drains corrode. Heavy use of drain cleaning fluid erodes pipes especially in the bend under the sink where the solvent can sit for a period of time.

Gap Tooth decided to go upstairs and examine the pipes. Just as he thought, the pipes were old and corrosion had already begun. He just had to move the process along more quickly. Today was Thursday. If he put some acid down those sinks today, the pipes would be ready to spring a leak by Saturday. Since he planned to be at High Ridge by Saturday noon, he could give the pipes some encouragement to leak at that time. He recognized that no plumbing job could be completed in just one day, so he would come back on Sunday to finish up.

The plan was coming together. Gap Tooth's work assured his return to High Ridge on Sunday, the day of the million dollar tournament.

That night Gap Tooth reported his day's activities to Angelo and gave assurance that all the technical ground work had been laid. There would be no trouble on that end.

Angelo gave him some front money from Vito and warned Gap Tooth to keep a low profile while at High Ridge. Gap Tooth was pleased that his work was appreciated. He looked forward to receiving the remainder of his money when the heist was pulled off. The only thing he didn't like was the wig and the awkward bridge work.

He had just one question, "How are we going to handle the two guards who are watching the dough?"

"Don't worry, Vito has taken care of that. On Sunday you are going to give the guards dis." Angelo held out a small bottle of liquid. "This stuff will give them the runs like they've never had 'em before. It really is very powerful. So don't go takin' any of it yourself," he laughed. "I can see it now. Two guys who've got to go and there ain't no place to go. The nearby cans are busted, no water is running in there and these guys got to go. Dey run to the nearest john--downstairs in the locker room and the money is alone. Dat's when you make the grab."

Gap Tooth smiled. It was a funny picture. Two overweight ex-cop security guards running to the nearest point of relief.

"Remember," continued Angelo. "timing is everything. Be here Saturday morning at ten o'clock and I'll go over the plan with you again. The driver will also be here. This heist is going to work, and we are going to have bucks to burn when we're done."

Gap Tooth smiled again. This would be fun. As he turned to leave, Angelo called after him. "No word of this heist to anyone, or you won't be around to spend the money, if you get my drift."

Gap Tooth looked at him evenly and said, "I'm a professional. You don't have to worry about me."

High Ridge
Saturday, May 30th

The meeting with Angelo and Nunzio went well and now Gap Tooth was at the High Ridge Country Club, ready to work. His first stop was at the receptionist's desk. "Here I am, back again at High Ridge. My boss really wants the course in top notch condition for tomorrow's game. He's afraid some areas may be too wet due to the rain and the sprinkler system. I also have to look at certain parts of the course that got soggy and reduce the sprinkling there."

"You have some conscientious boss. He runs a great business," stated the receptionist. "You were here the other day so you don't need my help."

She returned to the envelopes she was stuffing. "Oh," she said, "there's a big wedding starting now in the banquet hall. Try to stay out of the way of the guests, not that any of them will be golfing," she giggled.

"No problem. Other than being on the course, most of my work will be downstairs at the sprinkler controls. I'm goin' out to check the areas that my boss told me about. Hey, I don't see anyone out there."

"The course is closed today to prepare it for the match tomorrow. Do you want me to call the greens keeper and have him go with you?"

Gap Tooth replied almost too quickly, "No, I'll go out first and if I find a problem, I'll come in and get him." The last thing he wanted was to meet the grounds keeper who probably knew the man from Logrosso's very well. "Thanks for your help. One more thing, where can I get one of those carts to ride out there?"

"They are parked at the far end of the parking lot. Just take one and go." She was anxious to get back to her work.

"OK," Gap Tooth said, and turned away from the desk. He slipped into the two restrooms to add more acid to the sink drains. While he was there he went into a stall and adjusted his dental bridge. It was very uncomfortable and he could not wait to get rid of it. After that he went to the parking lot.

He spent about thirty minutes riding around the course trying to stay out of sight of the groundskeeper and his workers. Gap Tooth figured enough time had elapsed for the acid to finish making holes in the drain pipes, and by now the restrooms should be in use. As he approached the clubhouse, he heard loud music and laughter. It sounded like a good wedding.

Liz Lake and Muffy Nixon entered the ladies' restroom. They were both breathless after the last Lindy that the orchestra had played.

"I haven't danced like that in years. I'm so glad the orchestra is playing our kind of music," said Muffy. She was leaning over the sink trying to put some cool water on the back of her neck with a damp towel. The water was turned on strong to keep the flow cold. Meanwhile, Liz was washing her hands at the adjoining sink.

"I do love your dress, Muffy. That apricot chiffon is perfect with your silver Manolo sandals."

"You don't think the dress is too long? I really want the shoes to be seen."

Both women were looking down at Buffy's shoes, when water started running along the floor from under the sink. "Eek, my Manolos are getting soaked."

They ran from the restroom, leaving the water running. By the time they reported the problem, water was running under the door and out into the hallway.

Situated in the room below the restroom, Gap Tooth listened for a commotion and looked for water coming from above. There it was, water was running down the wall, and women were squealing above him. He dashed upstairs in time to see the two women hurrying down the hall to the banquet room. The receptionist was leaning over her desk listening to the noise and trying to figure out what was happening.

Gap Tooth told her that evidently there was a leak in the ladies' room and luckily he was here to fix it. No need to bother Carlo Logrosso on the weekend. He could handle it, and for being "Johnny on the spot" he said he should get a bonus.

The receptionist was thrilled that she did not have to start looking for a plumber at four o'clock on a Saturday afternoon. Even though it was the manager's responsibility, he relegated such chores to her. She thanked Gap Tooth who was turning toward the restrooms. "I'll have the Club Manager come to see the problem, and you can explain what has happened and what you plan to do to fix it."

"Thanks," he said and hurried away. Gap Tooth went to the men's room before he approached the problem in the ladies' room. He wanted to be certain that the men's room would be out of service, too. The men's room drain pipe looked very bad and a slow drip was starting. He took more acid from his tool box and poured it into the drain. Then he went to the ladies' room which by now had two inches of water covering the floor. He turned off the faucets and arranged himself under the sink. He had just removed the first drain pipe when the Club Manager arrived.

"What is going on here?" Monsieur Jacques demanded.

"Looks like a drain pipe eroded," said Gap Tooth, waving the pipe at him.

"How could that happen?"

"Well, I'll tell you. If the cleaners use a lot of drain cleaner and let it stand in the pipes, eventually the pipes corrode and you get a mess like this one."

"How soon can you fix it?"

"I'll need to get some parts. This is an old building and so is the plumbing. The parts may be difficult to get. Or else I'll have to put in all new drain pipes for this bathroom."

"Well, get to it. We need the plumbing working. Thank God the men's room is operating.

At that moment they heard cursing and swearing coming from the men's room. Stan Harrison appeared at the doorway, red-faced and flustered. His evening shoes were soaked and the legs of his tuxedo trousers were soggy. "That sink is leaking and it did a job on me," he sputtered.

"I'd better turn off the water to both of these rooms. Your guests will have to use someplace else," stated Gap Tooth.

"The nearest facilities are in the locker room. I'll get the receptionist to put up signs and direction arrows." With that the manager departed.

Gap Tooth removed all the drain pipes and began to measure for their replacements. Using his cell he made a phony phone call within hearing distance of the receptionist. "Is this Croton Plumbing Supply? OK, I need four drain pipes and all the hardware that goes with them. Here's the dimensions." As he continued his fake call, the manager approached him and waited impatiently. Finally, the call ended and Gap Tooth shook his head and faced the manager. "Not good news. They don't have the parts. It's already late. The other supply houses are closed. The best I can do is repair them on Monday morning."

"Look," he continued, "We have a two foot gap in all the drains. No sinks can be used. I'm just worried that the corrosion may have gone into your main drains and that could be a very big problem. I'd like to spend time tomorrow checking them out. When the supplies come in on Monday, I'll know exactly what needs to be done."

The club manager was fighting for composure. "All right," he finally said. "Do what you have to do. I'll devise some plan to meet the needs of today's guests and tomorrow's tournament attendees. By the way, how come you are willing to work tomorrow? A Sunday?"

"I'm the designated plumber on call for Logrosso this weekend. It's my job."

"Good. Do your job well…and thank you."

As Gap Tooth packed up his tools, he smiled to himself. "I am an amazing liar," he thought, "and a smart one. These money types are a pushover."

Neopolitan Club
Sunday, May 31st

Angelo was busy reading the Westchester Weekly when Gap Tooth arrived. Holding the newspaper clutched in his left hand, Angelo announced, "Now I know how you can easily get dat shit sauce into de guards. Once again 'Close Up with Colette' has come through for us."

" Today's column is all about the fancy hors d'oeuvres that a famous New York City chef is making to be served at the tournament. They are going to deliver these tidbits by golf cart to the people on the course. That's good for us because they will all run outside to get this gourmet food and there will be no one in the Clubhouse. The best part is the guards will want some of this food, too, and they cannot leave the money."

" So you," he said, smiling and pointing at Gap Tooth, "will have to get the food from the kitchen and bring it to them … with a little extra sauce." Then Angelo gave the small bottle to Gap Tooth.

Holding the bottle up to the light, Gap Tooth asked, "What is this stuff anyway?"

"Who knows? Vito got it from an old lady in Little Italy who makes special potions for the boys to use on special jobs. Also for any personal needs that they might have, if you get my drift."

Opening the door with a bang, Nunzio came stomping in with, "Sorry I'm late. I had to get de van painted with de Logrosso sign. It took forever to dry, but it's perfect."

"OK, let's get into our plumber's overalls and head for High Ridge. We know what we have to do, so let's do it."

High Ridge
Sunday, May 31st

The parking lot was already filled and it was only nine a.m. The twosomes were due to go off at eleven with Sunset Hills and High Ridge teeing off last. A free Continental breakfast was being served in the dining room, and club members munched on bagels and donuts. Everyone had passed by the bowl filled with one million dollars at least once, and many had been by twice.

The guards were keeping onlookers much farther away than they wanted to be. A little boy was crying because a guard had yelled at him for getting too close. Much earlier a picture had been taken with all the contestants clustered around the bowl, but the guards had made them move back the minute the pictures were done.

Jimmy Lawson was mingling with the members to make certain the day was running smoothly. The waitresses had started to clear the breakfast food. So far so good. Shortly they would be running complimentary food and drink out to various areas on the course. On this special day the guest chef was serving his signature hors d'oeuvres. They consisted of an exotic medley recently reviewed in Gourmet magazine.

"I'm glad I'm sober," thought Jim. "I never could've handled this with a few drinks in me." He had left Ted in the pro shop. People were buying sweaters and jackets right and left as the weather had unexpectedly turned cooler.

Jim had enlisted Betsy to be his 'gofer,' and she had a walkie-talkie. "Now if we can get through the tournament and then dinner with few mishaps it will be a good day." A committee of wives had done the decorations and even hired a disc jockey for dancing.

Jim had planned for the golfers to go directly from the course to the ballroom for dinner and the presentation of the money, but now it looked as though the women were requiring them to shower and change. "If I had my way we could just sit down and enjoy ourselves," groused Jim. "If the women had their way we would be in black tie."

The sixteen contestants were busy practicing both at the driving range and on the putting green. Hudson View had no chance of winning, but still put on a good "game face." Turtle Creek was just a long shot. High Ridge and Sunset Hills were tied for first place.

Hank, Peter, Connie and Brad had been practicing all week. They hoped they had the edge since this last contest was at their home course. The first three had won four points apiece and Brad, three. Connie was happy that Peter held up his second place position. There had been grumblings about Peter's playing so soon after his wife's death.

Connie thought that after this was all over, she might take Laura under her wing, either getting her interested in golf or the medical field. Connie had seen her drifting aimlessly for the past few years. Connie knew full well it was important to have someone guide you through the impressionable years. Thank God for Ben.

Speaking of Ben, she hadn't heard from Ed all week. She knew he had been taking night call quite a bit so his weekends were free for this tournament. Cliff, her medical partner, had been wonderful, taking a great deal of her call. He planned on a two week vacation so her "payback" was coming up.

Just then Jim made the announcement that the first group should be ready to tee off. As Connie turned to leave the putting green, she bumped into Ed coming up behind her.

"Hi, Connie. I apologize for not getting in touch, but we had some tough cases this week. I'll make it up to you though."

Connie thought it only took a minute to make a phone call, but she decided not to start a fight before their matches began. She was happy Hank was playing Ed and not she.

Finally it was time for High Ridge to tee off. Hank put a gorgeous drive down the left side of the fairway. There was a great deal of applause from the members. Ed stepped up, took a practice swing, and hit a booming drive five yards past Hank's. Another round of applause and the two walked down the fairway with their caddies.

Peter and his opponent hit perfect drives, also. For some reason, Peter's caddy, Sean, was not able to make it today. The substitute was capable, but a player and his caddy were somewhat like a marriage. Peter was not happy.

Then it was Connie's turn. Her opponent, Bill Haggerty, had lodged a complaint about Connie playing from the white tees while he had to play from the blue. He was referred to the rules of this particular tournament where the men were from the blues, and ladies, the whites.

This had irritated Connie, and she realized she had to put it behind her. This guy probably liked to play "head" games, and she needed to focus and play her own brand of golf.

Connie's gallery was mostly women. High Ridge was known as a "men's" club so the women enjoyed it when one of their own bested a man. Connie had the largest gallery so there was friendly jostling to see their drives.

Connie teed off and split the fairway down the middle. Her opponent sliced his drive into the right rough. He was completely closed out for a shot to the green. Jim Lawson had them move along so the last foursome could go off. He was pleased that everything was coming together.

The sun went under the clouds and the weather got colder. Rain was not forecast, but the clouds looked threatening. It didn't stop the members from following their favorite tournament player.

After nine holes Ed was leading Hank one up, Peter had his opponent two up, Connie was even, and so was Brad. None of the matches seemed to be a runaway.

High Ridge
Sunday Noon, May 31st

The white van with the Logrosso logo pulled into the High Ridge parking lot. The tournament had started at eleven and the parking lot was packed. Nunzio had to park at least two hundred yards from the front entrance. Angelo and Nunzio planned to wait in the van while Gap Tooth did his work.

Grunting under the weight, Gap Tooth hefted the extra large tool case out of the van and walked back to the front entrance.

He wanted to give the impression that he had come alone. In addition to plumbing tools, the bag also contained Don Vito's special sauce and hidden in the bottom was a canvas bag filled with phony money.

Angelo wanted to have as much get away time as possible.

At a distance, the phony money would look real when seen through the sparkling cut crystal, and no one would know it was not real until the presentation in the banquet room.

By the time Gap Tooth got to the front door, he was panting.

He felt like the piece covering his teeth would choke him.

That plumber's case was really heavy. There was no receptionist on duty. Security wanted as few people as possible around that cash filled urn. The two security guards looked up suspiciously as he entered.

Gap Tooth smiled at them and thought, "I was right, they are retired cops. One is fat, but the other is tall and skinny. They look like Abbott and Costello."

"Hi, guys. As you can see, I'm the plumber. I'm sure you've been told about the rest room disaster around the corner." The two guards nodded, sizing him up.

"You goin' to fix the crappers?" the fat one asked.

"Not today. Don't have the parts."

"Oh, shit. We've been here since eight o'clock when we brought the money in. Where do we have to go to take a piss?" the heavy one moaned.

"There's a bathroom in the locker room. Go into the hall on your left, walk to the end, go down a flight of stairs and you're in the locker room." Gap Tooth directed. The two guards seemed satisfied, but reluctant to leave the money.

Gap Tooth looked up at the urn placed on the pedestal. "Wow, that is some piece of glass!" The urn was three feet high and two feet across and sparkled in the light. It was filled with money. The green shone through the glass.

"Is that real money?" Gap Tooth asked.

"Sure is." responded the fat one. "That's why we're here. One million dollars in greenbacks."

"So if you're not going to fix the bathrooms today, why are you here?" asked the skinny guard, all business.

"There's a strong possibility some of the other pipes might leak. I'm here to check them out." Changing the subject, Gap Tooth added, "Did you hear about the gourmet chef that's making hors d'oeuvres for this golf bash? Seems they're sending hundreds of his tasty concoctions out on golf carts to the people watching the match."

"We could use a few of those. I'm starving," said the fat cop.

"Let me put my bag away downstairs and then I'll poke around and see if I can find us some grub." With that Gap Tooth picked up his case and took the stairs down to the control room. When he got there, he inserted the loop into the video camera so the urn would look undisturbed to anyone viewing the monitor. He took the bag of phony money out of the case and placed a wad of money – one thousand dollars in real fifty and twenty dollar bills – on top of it.

Then he slipped the shit sauce into his pocket, returned upstairs and headed for the kitchen. It was now close to one o'clock. Gap Tooth singled out a young waiter who looked too small for his tuxedo jacket.

Coming up behind him, Gap Tooth asked, "Any chance of getting some samples? The guards outside are starved."

The kid was startled to see Gap Tooth in the kitchen. He knew only kitchen staff were allowed in there. The Master Chef was very fussy. "I don't think I can give you anything," he stammered.

"Look, give me something that's not quite perfect, something slightly burned or not cut the way it should be. Something the Chef would not serve. Have a heart, those guys have been here since eight o'clock this morning with nothing to eat."

The kitchen was filled with delicious smells and rapidly moving people taking hors d'oeuvres on serving trays out to the ninth green.

Anxious to get rid of Gap Tooth, the waiter dumped a full tray of slightly burned jalapenos stuffed with cream cheese, another of soggy rumaki and a half tray of poorly cut sushi onto a huge serving platter. "I know this Chef would find these not suitable for our guests."

Gap Tooth took the tray mounded with thirty or forty pieces of food and left the kitchen. The bar was between the kitchen door and the foyer. Like every place else in the club house, the bar was empty. He placed the tray on the bar, put a jalapeno in his mouth, set two rumaki and three sushi aside and removed the bottle from his pocket. He uncorked the bottle, liberally sprinkled the jalapenos and the rumaki and put a large drop into the center of each piece of sushi. Then he poured two sodas and carried the tray and the drinks into the foyer.

"Here's to you guys. I'll be back in a minute to join you in this repast." The guards looked up at Gap Tooth in surprise. He set the tray and glasses on a table beside the fat guard and went back for his plate and soda.

When he got back, the guards had almost finished the hors d'oeuvres. "This chow tastes like shit. I guess rich people will eat anything," said the fat guard as he burped.

"I guess we'll eat anything, too," the skinny guard laughed as he showed a piece of sushi in his mouth. "Even raw fish."

Gap Tooth sat near them on a sofa and finished his plate and soda. "Yeah, I think it's awful, too, but I'm hungry. Let me take your glasses and the tray back to the kitchen. They were worried that the manager should know that we are eating the good stuff." The guards stuffed the last of the food into their mouths and handed him the tray with a muffled thanks.

When Gap Tooth returned to the foyer, the guards thanked him again and remarked that he was very nice to feed them. "More thoughtful than those rich slobs," the fat one burped.

"I gotta get back to work if I'm going to be home for early dinner. See ya." Gap Tooth headed for the stairs to the basement. He closed the plumber's case and put it under the bench. He put the satchel with the money near the door. Then he waited.

The guards sprawled in their chairs half dozing after the heavy food. Suddenly, the skinny one felt a sharp gas pain. He looked over at his partner who also seemed to be in distress.

They squirmed in their chairs then bolted for the bathroom downstairs in the locker room.

As soon as Gap Tooth heard them move, he grabbed the satchel and headed for the foyer. As he opened the door at the top of the stairs, he saw the guards entering the stairs at the far end of the hall. In seconds Gap Tooth was standing on the bench surrounding the pedestal.

The satchel lay open on the floor. He reached for the urn sitting on the pedestal. The base of the urn was level with his head. The urn was much heavier than he anticipated and it slipped and slid down his body as he tried to balance on the soft tufted bench. Somehow, he got it on to the bench.

Gap Tooth took an empty garbage bag from the satchel and shoveled handfuls of the real money from the urn into it. When that was completed, he dumped a plastic bag of phony money into the urn. He then removed a wad of real twenties and fifties from his pocket and scattered the real money over the top of the phony money.

Anyone looking into the urn would think the money was real all the way to the bottom. The cutting of the crystal prevented anyone looking from the side to determine if the money was real or not.

Gap Tooth closed the satchel and then proceeded to place the urn back on the pedestal. This was more difficult than taking it down. He had to get solid footing on the soft bench and then carefully loft this large heavy weight on to the eighteen inch wide pedestal. The urn was wider than the pedestal so it had to be placed dead center or it would tip over.

With one mighty heave, he got the urn over his head and on to the pedestal. It took a few seconds of maneuvering to center the urn, but finally it was safely in place.

Gap Tooth was still on the bench when he heard the guards coming back down the hall. He grabbed the satchel and headed for the door. He was down the outside steps and into the parking lot before the exhausted guards stumbled into the foyer.

Walking briskly he reached the van at the far end of the lot in less than a minute. He tossed his bag into the back of the van, telling Nunzio and Angelo everything had gone well. Removing his uncomfortable bridgework and hot wig, Gap Tooth climbed into the passenger side of the van and the trio sped away.

Golf Course
Sunday Afternoon, May 31st

The gallery was sampling all the food out at the course. Everyone was enjoying the party atmosphere. Jim was roving the course in his golf cart to see if any of the players needed rulings. He looked up at the sky and frowned.

"Betsy," said Jim over the walkie talkie, "Can you hear me?"

"Yes, Dad, what can I do for you?"

"You're close to the clubhouse. Go to the pro shop and ask Ted to give you the weather report off the computer. I'm on the tenth green and it looks threatening. I want some warning if the siren is going to go off."

"Sure, Dad, I'm pulling up to the clubhouse now." Betsy parked her golf cart and ran inside.

"Hi, Ted, my Dad wants to know what's happening with the weather."

Ted looked on the computer screen and said, "The rain is definitely coming, but I think we're going to avoid an electric storm. The contestants might have to play through some heavy rain, though. It just came up all of a sudden."

"Thanks, Ted." Betsy spoke into the walkie talkie. "Dad, come in. Darn, it doesn't seem to be working."

Ted replied, "That's probably the one that's temperamental. You're going to have to go out onto the course in person, Betsy. I'll tell you, it's like a ghost town in here. I can't believe the number of people out on the course."

"I know, Ted. I better run and tell Dad. See ya." Betsy hurried out to the cart and tried to drive away. Her cart was dead. "Speaking of temperamental," thought Betsy. "Nothing is working around here."

She went up to the starter and said, "Hey, Jeff. I need a new cart to go out to my Dad. Mine is dead."

"Betsy, the only cart left is in the parking lot. We were using it to ferry the contestants' clubs from their cars. You're welcome to it."

Betsy hurried out to the lot and spied the cart parked next to a white van. As she was putting the cart in reverse she noticed a man climbing into the van. He looked vaguely familiar. He had a huge gap between his two front teeth. She glanced again, but the van started to drive away. " I'd better get to my Dad," thought Betsy as she hurried off.

The rain held off for a few more holes. The Turtle Creek and Hudson View players had just finished, but not in the running.

Hank was one up on the back nine going into seventeen, a par three. The wind was blowing against them on this 165 yard hole.

Hank teed his ball up and decided on a six iron. He swung a little too hard because of the wind and landed in the left trap. Ed also took a six iron, but swung a little easier. His ball ended up eight feet from the hole.

When Hank arrived at the trap he saw that his ball was sitting up nicely. He was one of the best trap players at the club. Hank took his lob wedge and hit the ball within one foot. The crowd broke into loud applause.

Ed conceded Hank's putt and spent some time studying the line of his putt with his caddy. Finally he stepped up, took his stance and drilled the putt right into the hole for a birdie. The match was now even for the back nine.

Both men played good tee shots with three woods over the trees on eighteen. Ed was slightly behind Hank, and consulted with his caddy. He decided on another three wood and hit the perfect shot 20 feet from the pin.

Hank's ball had landed in a divot, and his caddy suggested he lay up before the brook. Hank disregarded his advice as he felt a five wood could make it to the green. He just managed to get over the water, however.

Hank "chili dipped" has third shot which did not get on the green. The pin was in the middle, and Hank chipped to within a foot for a bogey five.

All Ed had to do was lag a putt up to the hole, and he would win all three points. Pumped up with adrenalin, Ed went five feet past the hole. He wanted to hit himself in the head with his putter.

Ed calmed down, telling himself he was an excellent putter and five feet was nothing. Confidently he stood over the putt and sunk it. Three points!

Peter came in for High Ridge with three points so the contest now came down to Connie and Brad. Brad actually came up to the eighteenth hole before Connie. Bill Haggerty had lost a ball on fourteen so Brad's group had played through while they were looking for it.

Both Brad and his opponent parred eighteen to finish tied. That left Connie. By this time the wind had really whipped up. The lost ball stayed lost, so Connie's opponent gave her the hole. She was now one up. A runner for the High Ridge team had managed to convey that the match was tied so it was up to Connie.

Hole fifteen was lined with trees, making the fairway landing very narrow. Connie teed off and hooked her drive into the trees while Bill hit a gorgeous drive down the middle.

Connie found herself behind a tree, and the only shot she had was to chip out sideways. Her third shot landed on the green for a one-putt and par, but Bill had birdied. All even.

Sixteen was a straight short par four and both got down in par. By now there was a huge crowd around the seventeenth green. The wind was blowing so fiercely that Bill took a five iron. The wind pushed his ball into the right trap.

Connie took a wood and hit her shot over the green. It bounced, hit an onlooker, and dropped into rough so deep you could not see the ball.

Connie was away and barely got her ball on the green about thirty feet from the hole. Bill blasted out of the sand nicely and had a two foot putt for par. He had a big smile on his face thinking he would be one up going into eighteen.

Connie walked around the green once looking at the slant. She stepped up, put a nice stroke on the ball and watched it roll from right to left slowly towards the hole. It was a downhill putt and started to pick up momentum just when she thought it was going to stop. It started to curl around the hole and then, plop, fell in. The crowd went wild. Bill proceeded to hole out his ball and they went to eighteen tied.

Bill sailed his ball over the trees on eighteen into a little swale. Connie chose to go down the fairway which meant she might have to lay up before the water. Unfortunately her tee shot did not make it to the severe bend so her second shot was short of the water. Connie was laying two to Bill's one.

Now they were faced with the severe elevation. By now the rain had started and most of the crowd had gone inside. Connie's club slipped in her hands and hit the right side of the green. A yell of approval came from the few people remaining, but Connie knew it had gone to the back of the green even though she could not see it.

Bill took his swing and watched his ball sail in a beautiful arc right towards the flag. He heard someone say, "It's in the hole." By now the rain was coming in torrents. Bill ran up to the green and saw his ball one inch from the hole. He pulled out the flag and tapped it in.

"No," shouted one of the lone spectators. "You hit one inch before the hole and rolled to the back. We thought it was going in the hole on the fly. See your pitch mark?" The indentation of Bill's ball was a half inch just slightly to the left side of the hole.

Connie got up to the green. The same spectator told her that her ball had hit the hill on the right side of the green and was deflected to the left, almost going in the hole.

"I put your ball in the hole," said Bill in disbelief. "In match play I lose the hole." Bill and Connie had tied the front for one-half point each, but Connie had won the back and overall for a total of two and a half points.

Connie said, "I'm truly sorry, Bill. I really didn't want to win this way." Her mind clicked that their team had won the million dollars. Where are my wimpy teammates, she wondered? Just because we can't see in front of us due to the driving rain is no reason they can't be out here. Just then the three men came running out of the pro shop, giving her high fives and hugs.

The foursome was dripping wet when they walked inside. "Ed wanted me to tell you he had to go and see a patient, Connie," said Brad. "He really was interested in how you finished, and not because of his own team. I like him not only as a doctor, but as a person." Then

Brad found the two dozen red roses Ed had left for her and gave her the flowers.

Connie was overwhelmed by this generosity. No one had ever been this romantic. He just might be a keeper, she thought. Everyone decided they had better take showers and change into dry clothes.

First, they wanted to see their money, however. When they went into the foyer, the million dollars had already been transferred to the ballroom. "At least there were no mishaps with the money," Brad said.

"Maybe we need to hire the guards to take us home in their armored truck," joked Connie. They agreed to meet outside their respective locker rooms after getting dressed.

"Don't take too long getting gussied up, Connie," said Hank. "You're already pretty enough."

"Is that a southern term, Hank? I think my grandfather used to say that."

"Honey chile, I'm not your grandpa, but if you want to sit on my lap, I'll read you a story." Hank went over and put his arm around Connie.

"Sorry, Hank, I'm too wet and you're too married. See you in fifteen minutes." Both locker rooms were empty as everyone was showered, dressed, and headed for the ballroom.

Connie took a quick shower and turned on the hair dryer. She had her roses propped up on a chair. Looking critically in the mirror she decided that her chestnut hair, now shiny clean, was one of her best attributes. *Maybe I'll let it grow even longer.*

She pictured Ed running his fingers through her hair. *Enough daydreaming*, she thought. *The men are probably waiting.* She broke off a rose and stuck it in her hair. With her clingy black top and tight pants she was bound to turn heads. Connie was hoping Ed would get back in time.

As it turns out the men had opened a bottle of champagne and taken a sauna after showering . The locker room attendant, Joe, brought her out a glass from her partners. *It's a testosterone-filled world,* thought Connie disgustedly.

Then an idea burst into her head. The sauna was situated between the men's and women's locker room which was reached from either side. A door between the two was locked on the men's side so no one could accidentally enter the wrong part. Joe had just started to go back inside.

"Wait, Joe. Here's a fifty to open the door between the saunas. You can lock it again in twenty minutes."

Joe pocketed the fifty and winked as he went back inside. Connie went back into the locker room, took off her clothes, and wrapped in a towel entered the now unlocked door. She opened the men's sauna, and hoisting her glass of champagne said, "Here's to us, gentlemen. I understand we are starting the celebration in here." The men, dumbfounded, scrambled for their towels.

"Touche, Connie," responded Hank. "Join the party. I'm covering up so you're not disappointed in Ed."

"You mean you're covering up so Connie doesn't laugh hysterically," stated Brad. The four finished two bottles of champagne, Connie went back to the women's side and they were to meet as before in front of the locker rooms.

Connie and Peter were the first out. Peter took Connie by the arm and sat her down on the sofa. "Connie, before the others are here there's something I'd like to say." He looked intently into her eyes.

"I don't **want** this to seem inappropriate. Both Laura and I have to mourn. It won't be for awhile, but I'd like to see you as a friend, or whatever else it might lead to. Gloria and I had gone our separate ways for a long time. We had become strangers."

"You seem to have a loving nature which would be good for both Laura and myself. Sorry, I don't know why I'm saying this now. I've had a little too much champagne."

Connie took Peter's hand in both her own and said, "Peter, I'm chalking up your speech to the champagne. I'm very flattered at what you said, but I know you're just lost in grief now. Concentrate on Laura--she needs you."

Brad and Hank came out chuckling at Connie's audacity, and the four walked into the ballroom. The crowd gave them a standing ovation. Millie, Laura, Sarah, Stephanie and Chad were already seated at their table. All the other tables were filled. Even those teams who had lost were excited to see one million dollars in cash being given away.

Ed had just arrived, escorting a gorgeous silver-haired woman.

He came up to Connie and introduced his mother, Claudia, by saying, "I'd like two beautiful women to meet each other."

Ed's mother said, "You must be a very special person, Constance. I've rarely heard such high praise from Ed." Introductions were made around to the rest of the group, and then Ed and Claudia took their seats at the next table.

Ed had time to whisper, "I'd like to see you later."

While dessert was being served, Jim came up to the microphone. He was standing by the bowl containing the million dollars. Both guards had backed away. "Welcome contestants, their families and friends. It is my distinct pleasure to award this bowl and its contents to High Ridge. Would the contestants and their families please come up."

Stephanie being the youngest had skipped up quickly to the bowl. It was easy to see she was very excited. Before anyone could stop her she dipped into the bowl with both hands and threw some of the money in the air. "Mommy, Hank, it's play money. Did they get it from a Monopoly game?"

Everyone close by rushed over to the bowl. "Robbery!" someone shouted from the crowd.

One of the guards yelled, "No one leave this room." Pandemonium had struck and no one listened to the guard. They ran for the exits in case they would be robbed next.

The two guards stepped back and started whispering. One said to the other, "You know we're dead meat if we admit we left the money."

The other agreed and said, "No matter what, admit nothing. I wonder when it was done?"

"Don't be stupid. That guy that gave us the food must have put something in it to give us the runs. Then he copped the money. We'd better call our boss."

Hank picked up some of the money. Most of it was play money, but there were a few real twenties and fifties. He looked at the guards who seemed stupefied and asked, "Did you leave the bowl with the money at any time?" The two guards looked at each other before one of them said, "No, we have no idea when a switch was made."

Peter said in a low voice to Hank, "Maybe this was an inside job. I don't know if anyone has called the police yet, but I'm dialing my cell phone now."

"911. State your emergency," the operator said.

"This is Peter Drummond. We've had a million dollars in cash stolen from the High Ridge Country Club. You had better send someone over fast." He hung up the phone as the guards were still trying to stop people from leaving the ballroom.

Stephanie was clinging to Sarah. "I'm really scared, Mama."

"It's alright, Stephanie," soothed Sarah as she stroked her hair.

"You were very smart to let us know the money wasn't real. The police have been called, and they will find out who did it."

She looked over Stephanie's head at Hank for verbal reassurance. Hank put his arm around both Stephanie and Sarah. "Don't worry, Steph. We are very safe. They'll find out who took the money. If they don't, the Safety Assured Company has insurance and we'll be paid off. If you want a baby grand piano as your part of my money, then you can have it."

Stephanie put her arms around Hank and gave him a kiss. Sarah looked grateful and took Hank's hand. Chad looked at his father and said, "Gee, Dad, if you're handing out gifts I wouldn't mind a car. I get tired of Laura driving me around."

"A car costs a little more than a piano, Chad. We'll look at your grades and then decide."

Millie leaned over to Brad and said, "We'd better call the children and let them know we're OK. Who knows when the TV reporters will get wind of it. Knowing Collette she's probably on her way over now. We'll surely be in her column this week."

One of the guards came up to their group and suggested they all go back to their table and sit down. Several squad cars had already arrived. Ed came over and hugged Connie.

"Connie, my mother is very upset. The minute we can leave, I'm taking her home. I'd still like to see you later. I have something important that I would like to talk to you about."

"Ed, I'd like to see you, too. By the way, I haven't thanked you for the roses yet. What a romantic thing to do."

"I'm a sentimental guy, Connie. My parents were very much in love, and my Dad always tried to show my Mom how much he cared for her. I'd like to do that for you."

Just then Peter came up behind Connie. "The guards want us to sit at our own tables. The police will be questioning us one on one. I can't imagine we'll be suspects since we won the money. The quicker we cooperate, hopefully the quicker we'll get the money back."

Ed kissed Connie on the cheek and went back to his table.

"Are you serious about him, Connie?" asked Peter.

"I've only known him a short time, Peter. We've just started to date."

"He seems like a great guy. Maybe I'm doomed before I even begin."

"Peter, I'll always be your friend. And I'd really like to take Laura under my wing. She's a good athlete and maybe we could work on getting her a soccer scholarship."

"That's wonderful, Connie. She's going to need a woman's touch. I think Gloria and I let her grow up with too much freedom."

"You can still be a parent, Peter. I heard Chad and Laura were dating, but she wouldn't even look at him at the table."

"You know more than I do, Connie. I'll keep an eye on that relationship." Peter ushered her into her chair and took a seat beside Laura.

What was running through Peter's mind was that he was in serious trouble. The loan shark expected his money first thing tomorrow and Peter wouldn't have it. He wondered if he should approach Chip. Maybe that wouldn't look so good, if he were starting a job with Chip's law firm.

Laura took his hand and said, "This is rather exciting, Dad. Who do you think stole the money? Do you think it was the guards?"

"I don't know about that, Laura, but they sure are in plenty of trouble."

Officer Morrissey came to their table first. "I'm just going to ask you each a few specific questions, but let me say you are the least likely to have stolen your own money." Within a half hour everyone at the table was cleared and left for home.

The minute someone yelled robbery, Betsy had wheeled her mother out of the ballroom. Since her dad was at the podium he wouldn't be able to help them escape. They could, however, as their table was situated by the door. Knowing the country club quite well, she hid with her mother in a little-known linen closet. It was the size of a small room and housed all the extra china, linen and glasses. Betsy felt if anyone with guns was still in the club they wouldn't look in here, especially with the door locked.

"Mom, what do you think we should do?" Betsy was terrified a gang of thieves would burst into the ballroom at any minute and harm her father.

"Betsy, I think the money was stolen awhile ago. The thieves are probably long gone. It looks like it might've been an inside job. I'm going to call your Dad on his cell and see what is going on."

Jim's cell rang three times before he picked it up. "Ann, where are you? I've been so worried. The police are here and won't allow anyone to leave."

Just then the doorknob rattled on the closet door, followed by, "Police. Open this door."

Betsy looked at her Mom, questioning. "Do as he says, Betsy. Your dad said the police are here so we are safe." Betsy ran to the door and opened it. The officer turned out to be the one who on off duty hours patroled the country club.

"Oh, it's you Mrs. Lawson, and Betsy. I'm supposed to be questioning everyone I come across concerning the stolen money, but I'm not worried about you. Here's a pass to let you go through the police barricade."

"Thank you Officer McConnell. I really would like to get home. When do you think my husband will be released?"

"I'll check that out for you ma'am." The officer got on his walkie talkie. "Officer Morrissey, I have Mrs. Lawson and Betsy Lawson here, and I've cleared them. Do you know when Mr. Lawson will be allowed to go?" The officer heard talking in the background.

"McConnell, Jim Lawson says he wants to stay and try to straighten things out, if possible. He wants you to tell his wife and daughter to go home. I'll actually send them home in a squad car if they'd like."

Officer McConnell looked at Ann and asked if they'd like a ride.

"Thank you, officer, but as you can see I need a van that will fit a wheelchair. I'm all set with my own transportation."

The officer looked embarrassed as though he'd made a gaffe. He held the door open so they could exit the linen closet. When they got out to the parking lot, Betsy remembered the white van she had seen with that familiar-looking fellow. She thought about running back inside to tell someone, but she felt her mother was awfully pale and needed to get home.

Once they arrived home Betsy took the portable phone from the hallway and went to her room. While most girls would have a feminine-looking room, Betsy's was very simple and uncluttered. Her grandmother's quilt graced the bed and her favorite childhood bear, Neddybelle, was propped on the window seat. It had one eye, and was losing its stuffing.

Ann kept trying to redo the room with Betsy's approval, but Betsy was not into material things. A Degas poster of a ballerina was hung on the wall behind the bed, put up when Betsy went through her dance phase at the age of eight. She was actually quite good and performed in a Lincoln Center version of the Nutcracker. The only other wall hanging was the framed letter. It stated that Betsy was the recipient of a full academic scholarship to Turner Academy High.

Betsy leaned back on her pillow and dialed the LaGrange home. She was hoping Chris would pick up and not his mother or father. Betsy felt relieved when she heard Chris's voice.

"Chris, it's Betsy. Did you hear what happened at the club tonight?"

"Hi, Bets. How nice to hear your voice. I've been hitting the books all day so haven't heard anything. What's going on? I know our team won the money. Chad called me with that info. Did they distribute it tonight?"

"Chris, it was stolen. Stephanie was the first up to the bowl, and she dipped her hands in the money. It was counterfeit or should I say play, like you find in a board game. The police are swarming all over the club."

"Oh my gosh. Do they have any idea who did it? I thought the guards were watching it the whole time."

"Some people are speculating that it's an inside job. But Chris, I wanted to ask you. Do you remember that guy with a big gap between his front teeth that stopped by your house? He said he was checking your sprinkler system, but it ended up he was at the wrong house? Well, I saw him this afternoon in the parking lot of the club. He was getting into a white van with a sign that said Logrosso. Do you think I should tell the police? Maybe that time he was at your house he was casing it, too."

Chris was shocked. The last thing he needed was Gap Tooth being interrogated by the police. Definitely he would involve Chris with the

Putting for the Green

coke. "Betsy, don't say anything to anybody. I happen to know the Logrosso Company, and they do repair sprinklers. They were probably doing repair work on the course. My Dad is a friend of the owner. I'll have him check it out."

Betsy seemed a little dubious, but didn't want to get on the wrong side of Chris. "O.K., Chris, but do ask your Dad. It would make me feel better. I need to check up on my Mom now. Talk to you later."

"I'm glad you called, Betsy. I haven't been able to get you out of my mind all day. I'm just about finished studying. I want to take you to a nice restaurant for dinner to thank you for your help on the project."

"Lenny's pizza is fine with me, Chris. It was where we had our first date. Bye."

Chris was startled to find he really dug Betsy. "She's the opposite of all the girls I've dated, but she's perfect for me," he thought. "Oh my God, I got distracted for a minute. What am I going to do about Gap Tooth? He probably was involved in some way."

One thing Chris didn't understand was why Gap Tooth was in a Logrosso truck. He was a mechanic, not a plumber. Chris put his head in his hands--what to do?

His one conclusion, as hard as it might be, was to tell his Dad. His Dad actually had no idea that Chris had discovered a few years ago that their last name, LaGrange, was actually changed from Logrosso. Chris was a whiz on the internet and had Googled this information.

He also knew his father's brother owned the Logrosso Plumbing Company. He never knew why his father had kept all this a secret. Maybe he was ashamed of his family. That didn't seem like his Dad though. Chris hoped he would get home soon.

It was several hours before Vincent and Valerie walked in the door. Chris had been fidgeting in the great room for the past thirty minutes thinking about what he must do.

"Dad, could you come in the den for a minute? I really need to speak to you."

"Do we have another problem, Chris? I thought we were done with all that nonsense. I've been very impressed with your grades lately. Has this something to do with your schoolwork? Do you need a tutor?"

"Wait, Dad. It has nothing to do with school. Will you sit down and listen? I know this isn't going to make you happy, but I'm in serious trouble."

Vincent sat down in his favorite chair. He thought that so far they've taken care of all the major problems so they should be able to solve one more. "Shoot, son. What else has happened? Did Betsy break up with you?"

Chris raised his voice. "Dad, please, just listen. It does involve Betsy, but let me tell you the whole story." Chris paced in front of his father.

"The night I came home slightly stoned, I had tried some coke that had been given to me. I got into a bad situation by banging up my car. When I tried to have it fixed without your knowing, I couldn't pay the price the mechanic quoted. He told me if I sold some coke for him he wouldn't charge me as much."

"I didn't know what to do so I agreed. Then Chad's house was raided by the police so I dumped a thousand dollars worth of cocaine into the pool chemicals. The mechanic wants his money."

Without warning Vincent slapped Chris across the face. "No son of mine will ever deal drugs. Do you understand me? Next time I'll turn you in myself." Vincent lifted his hand as if to strike him again, but stopped.

Chris cringed. "Dad, I'm so sorry. I felt like I had no where to turn. I know it was wrong and I promise I'll never do it again. But I need to finish my story. This mechanic that I call Gap Tooth was at the golf course today. Betsy saw him driving away in a plumbing truck that said Logrosso on the side. He also had a plumbing uniform on. But he's not a plumber, he's a mechanic."

Vincent looked dumbfounded. "You're sure the truck said Logrosso?"

"Dad, I know the owner is your brother. Could he have been involved in stealing the money? I made Betsy promise not to tell anyone because if they question Gap Tooth, I know he'll implicate me."

Vincent asked, " Chris, what are you talking about? What money was stolen?"

"You haven't heard? The million dollar pot was taken. No one knows who did it. The police questioned everyone at the tournament dinner."

Vincent asked some specific questions including where Gap Tooth worked. He ignored the fact that Chris knew about his brother. "Don't say anything to anyone, Chris. Tell Betsy I'm handling it. Hopefully everything will be OK. I have to think about this. You go on to bed." With that Vincent left the room.

The Carson Townhouse
Sunday, Late Evening, May 31st

Connie wearily climbed up the steps to her townhouse. She had dropped Peter and Laura at their home since Laura's car battery was dead. It was raining too hard to stand outside and charge the battery.

She decided to open a nice bottle of red wine. It had been too long a day. She pulled some cheese and salami out of the refrigerator and rummaged in the cupboard for crackers. Their victory dinner had been cancelled.

Connie settled on the sofa after putting on a Nora Jones CD. She snuggled under her afghan and took a long swallow of wine. Musing over the days event's, she decided it was good to be done with the tournament. It had taken its toll with everyone. Then the doorbell rang.

Ed was standing outside under an umbrella. "Can you let a drowned rat in?" Ed shook out his umbrella and left it by the front door. "I saw someone building an ark down the way. Have you seen any animals, two by two? This has been the rainiest month in history."

Ed sat down on the sofa and picked up the bottle of wine Connie had opened. "Jordan. You're a real wine maven, Connie."

Connie placed a Reidel glass before Ed.

"Ed, I can't quite believe what happened today. It was surreal."

"Yes, Connie, but you should be happy your team won. You actually determined that your team had the victory."

"I don't even feel as though I won, Ed. If Bill Haggerty hadn't hit the wrong ball on the last hole, who knows what would've happened?"

"There were seventeen other holes, Connie, and if it's comforting you need, I'm here now." Ed put his arms around her and nuzzled her hair. Connie felt a shiver go through her.

"Connie, your hair's a little damp from the rain and you feel cold. Why don't you pop in the shower, and I'll start a fire in the fireplace. Even though it's May, it feels like December."

"Great idea, Ed. I won't be long." Connie went into her bedroom, happy that she had made her bed and tidied up before the tournament. She slipped off her clothes and turned on the shower, filling the room with heat. Pushing the curtain aside, she climbed in and let the jets pulse over her body. A few minutes later the curtain parted again and Ed stepped in behind her.

"Like your back soaped, Connie?" Ed acted as though there was nothing unusual about having a joint shower with her. He soaped her back up well, and let his hands glide over the area, resting lightly on her buttucks.

Connie knew he was waiting for her decision. She turned around and playfully grabbed the soap. "My turn, Buster, and don't think it's just going to be your back." She started with his neck and broad shoulders. He had closed his eyes and was leaning back against the shower stall. His erection was already prominent.

She moved to his stomach and washed that thoroughly. Now she was feeling the heat, not just from the hot water. A delicious, anticipatory feeling came over her whole body. She knew this was the man who would be her destiny.

Connie's previous sexual experiences were few. She had been too busy becoming a cardiologist and also working to pay the medical school loans. She had been semi-serious about a med student, but when she heard via the grapevine he considered her a "sport-fuck," she dropped him instantly.

"Hey," Ed murmured as he took the soap away. "My turn again." This time he soaped all the intimate places, starting with her breasts. Then he moved to her pubic area and cupped her, moving his hand slowly. She immediately came.

Ed smiled, opened the shower curtain and grabbed a condom he had placed on the sink. Quickly sliding it on, he picked her up slightly, and holding her against him, slipped inside. He knew she would be wet from her orgasm. She put her legs around his waist and started naturally rocking. Her back was against the wall as he thrust into her.

"Oh, yes," he shouted, as he also came. She slid off and he gave her a deep kiss. They kissed and stroked each other until he became hard again. "The water's starting to turn cold. Let's adjourn to the bedroom."

As they dried each other off, Ed looked into Connie's eyes and said, "Connie, I wanted to say this before we made love. I'm crazy about you, and want to marry you. I hoped for some romantic setting, but I want you to know my intentions are honorable. I wasn't even going to use a condom because I wanted us to get married right away and start babies, but I didn't know if you felt the same way."

"Ed, I love you, too, and yes, I'd like to get married and have your babies. In that order." Just then the doorbell rang. They both looked at each other with apprehension. "Let's get dressed quickly. Whoever it is, sees both our cars outside."

The doorbell rang again as Ed stuffed his shirt into his pants and slipped on his loafers. Connie slipped a dress over her head and went to answer the door. She realized when she opened it that both Ed's and her hair were wet.

Hank stood at the front door. "Can I come in, I'm sopping wet with no umbrella." Connie ran to get him a couple of towels as Hank dripped on the floor. Hank looked into the living room and saw Ed sipping a glass of wine.

"Oh, hi, Ed. I hope I'm not interrupting anything. You look pretty cozy."

"Actually, Hank, we didn't hear the doorbell because we were both attempting to dry our hair and the dryers were noisy. We got soaking wet, too." By that time Connie had come back with towels and a pink chenille robe.

"Hank, why don't you step into the guest bathroom and change into this. That's where Ed was drying his hair so you'll find a hair dryer in there. I'll stick your clothes in the clothes dryer." Connie had heard Ed talk about the hair dryers and was happy Ed was quick-thinking. Maybe Hank didn't know what they had been doing.

Hank knew full well what had been going on. They both had the look of sex about them. However, he was on an important mission and couldn't afford to antagonize Connie.

Quickly he changed in the bathroom and came out looking ludicrous in the pink robe. Connie took his wet clothes and stuck them in the dryer. "Sit down and have a glass of wine, Hank," said Connie as she put out a third glass. "Pink is really your color," she said teasingly.

Hank practically gulped down his first glass of wine and held out his glass for more. "Connie, I know we've sometimes been at odds, but I'm sorry about that. I need your backing now. There is a grass roots action to oust me as club president because the money was stolen. They say the ultimate responsibility lies with me. I know I hired Safety Assured, but they had a phenomenal track record until now. What can I do?" he asked in an anguished tone.

"What did Jim Lawson say?" asked Connie. "He's our golf guru."

"The rest of the Board says it has nothing to do with Jim. They want a special meeting of all the club members to vote on taking away my presidency."

Ed couldn't understand what the big deal was, but didn't voice that out loud. Connie said, "I don't know how they can blame you, Hank. It was the guards watching over the money who goofed. Maybe the company, what's it called, Safety Assured, might have stolen the money themselves. Have you talked to Peter or Brad?"

"No, Connie, I came to you first. I'm going to both their homes now. You've made me much more comfortable about what happened."

Connie couldn't resist teasing Hank, however, and said, "Just don't wear that chenille robe at the meeting. I'll be there to support you ."

Connie retrieved Hank's clothes from the dryer, loaned him an umbrella and basically pushed him out into the night. Then she curled up next to Ed and asked, "Where were we?"

Hank proceeded to call both Peter and Brad from his cell phone, but only reached their answering machines. He decided to head on home.

Don Vito's Home
Sunday, May 31st

Vito was seated, as usual, behind his massive desk. He raised his head as his housekeeper opened the door for Angelo who was holding the satchel bearing the Logrosso logo, securely at his side.

"Come in," smiled the Don. Angelo was pleased with himself, but too smart to let it show. He smiled at Don Vito and placed the satchel on his desk.

"This is the fruits of our labors," he said quietly.

Don Vito left his chair and approached Angelo. He held Angelo by the shoulders and looked into his eyes. He liked what he saw: intelligence, confidence and a hint of wariness. The Don knew that he was right to keep Angelo out of sight during the heist. Angelo was a man of great promise.

"You did well, Angelo," he said gesturing at the bag.

"Now tell me all about the grab, in detail."

It was after nine o'clock when Angelo left the Sericusa residence. He could see Rosie and the kids in a nice house in a good neighborhood and himself as Don Vito's right hand man.

Someday. He hoped. Someday.

The Thunderbird Garage
Monday, Eight a.m., June 1st

Usually an early riser, Gap Tooth had slept late. The past few days had been stress-filled, but fun. He totally enjoyed conning people and he had done an excellent job of that to the members and staff of the High Ridge Country Club. What gullible types they were, he reflected. They were really easy to fool.

He stretched on his narrow bed in his room above the garage.

His take from the heist was hidden in an old suitcase in the corner of his room. In a few weeks he planned a long vacation, but not too soon. He did not want to attract attention by his sudden departure.

Besides, he had things to attend to. Two hundred thousand dollars plus interest had to be collected from Peter Drummond. It was due today. He planned to wait until tomorrow to collect it, just to build up more anxiety in Peter. Gap Tooth could not believe that Peter was one of the winners in the golf tournament.

The stolen money could have paid his debt. The guy must be frantic. Gap Tooth smiled.

Then there was his drug business. That LaGrange kid owed him for one thousand dollars street value of cocaine. It was weeks ago that that deal was made and broken. The kid must think he's off the hook – wrong! That dope was Gap Tooth's investment. The kid owed him.

Gap Tooth would tend to him as soon as he finished with Drummond. Don Vito was anxious to get his investment in Peter returned. So tomorrow is Peter Drummond day.

Putting for the Green

Gap tooth stumbled down to the garage. He hoped that the owner had made coffee. Yes, he had. A good strong cup was what Gap Tooth needed to start his day.

The LaGrange Home
Monday, Eight a.m., June 1st

Vincent sat at the kitchen table, his breakfast untouched. Last night's discussion with Chris had shaken him. He loved his son deeply. He was hurt that the boy feared him and did not tell him about the damaged car. The fact that Chris was so scared and foolish as to cover up the repair cost by pushing drugs was beyond his comprehension.

On top of all that, Chris has also told his father that he had searched the family history on the web and knew he was a Logrosso, not a LaGrange. What a mess.

Vincent appreciated his son's courage in reporting Betsy's sighting Gap Tooth in the country club lot. Still, his actions must be dealt with, but that would come later.

Now Vincent must act to protect his son and the Logrosso and LaGrange names. Vincent had no contact with his brother Carlo, and he intended to keep it that way. He wanted to distance himself from his father's shadowy reputation and be accepted for who he is and what he had accomplished.

Early that morning Vincent began to outline a plan to prevent his son's being connected to drug use and distribution. Vincent also wanted the Logrosso name clear of mob connection and the LaGrange name out of the picture.

By nine o'clock Jackson was driving Vincent to New York City in the limo. Vincent sat back and reflected on his life. He got a lucky break when his aunt took him out of his gang related neighborhood in

Brooklyn and moved him to Long Island. He had his mother to thank for that.

Vincent thrived in his new environment and over the years became a successful businessman. Now was the time for him to use the extensive profits of his success to do good and punish evil.

As they approached the city, Vincent outlined his plan to Jackson who was ready to cooperate. As Vincent had been saved, so had he done the same for Jackson by taking him from an unsavory neighborhood. Jackson loved Chris and would do anything to protect him and the LaGrange family.

By two o'clock Vincent was back home, and Jackson was preparing for what had to be done.

The Neopolitan Club
Monday, June 1st, 11a.m.

Don Sericusa's black limousine pulled up in front of the social club. His driver opened the door for him to exit. Nunzio and Nicky, who were standing outside, came forward and ushered the Don inside.

A long narrow table was set in the center of the room.

Various members of Vito's gang were seated around it. All stood when the Don entered. Each came forward to greet him. Vito took his place at the head of the table and all were seated.

The Don heard reports on his various "businesses". All seemed to be going well. Finally, the Don rose and stated that he had some announcements to make. He told them of the successful one million dollar heist in great detail. The men reacted appropriately. Then he thanked Big Carmine for training Angelo DeAngelo so well.

Angelo could run rings around Carmine any day, Vito thought, but he must save Big Carmine's face. From now on, the Don stated that Angelo was no longer reporting to Carmine.

Angelo now reports directly to Don Vito. There were murmurs of surprise and a smattering of applause. Angelo smiled and thanked Don Vito, careful not to let his elation show.

Big things were coming Angelo's way. He could feel it and he was ready.

The Hawthorne Home
Monday Afternoon, June 1st

When Hank came home early from work he found ten messages on the answering machine, mostly irate ones. The members felt as though the money being stolen at their club put them in a difficult position.

As he entered the front door, he was accosted by Chad. "Dad, how can you buy Stephanie a piano and not buy me a car? I'm your own flesh and blood and she's just a stepdaughter. I've been wanting a car for two years now. I had to take the school bus home today. Do you know how demeaning that is?"

"Chad, have you ever thought about earning money to help buy a car? I know you can't work during the school year, but last summer you were one big slug. I think you got up at eleven every day and then watched television. Stephanie is only ten years old and works very hard at her piano lessons."

"Yeah, but I'm the oldest and I think that makes me deserving of wheels. You always favor Sarah and Stephanie. You're really mean. No wonder Mom left."

"Well, she didn't take you with her. You're free to go anytime you want. Maybe her freeloader boyfriend will buy you a car. He makes so much money running a surf shop. Of course, he uses your Mom's alimony."

"Mom said I can go out to live with her whenever I want. I just wanted to finish school first. Maybe I'll go out there this summer."

"Be my guest. I don't like threats, Chad. Call your Mom tonight if you want. Do it on my nickel." With that Hank went into the great room and opened up the bar. He poured a stiff bourbon and downed half of it.

He knew Sarah was in her studio as the housekeeper had told him. All he wanted to do was relax with his drink and watch the boob tube. He probably had been too hard on Chad, but it was such a struggle with that kid. He was sure Chad felt abandoned by his mother. She seldom called. Maybe he would buy him a car, a secondhand one.

Chad had already gone upstairs and locked his door. He would've liked to smoke a little weed, but he was all out. He happened to have found a hundred in Sarah's studio yesterday, part of twenty-five hundred in cash she had just received for a portrait. He felt a foray into the drug world was needed.

" Maybe Laura will drive me there," he thought. He dialed her cell phone number and waited.

After a long time Laura picked up the receiver. "Hello."

"Hi, Laura, it's me. Would you like to pick me up and we'll head out for a little weed? Maybe we could hit Lenny's Pizza after and then stop at the lake. What do you think?" Chad could just picture smoking a joint and then having some exciting sex with Laura. Charleen was a great lay, but he thought he probably loved Laura.

At least he would love her until starting college next fall. Maybe if it wasn't too late he might look into colleges near his Mom. For sure no one cared what he did in this house.

There was silence on the other end of the phone. Then the tirade began. "Chad, haven't you figured out yet that we are no longer a couple? If you were the last person on earth I wouldn't date you. You are a selfish, inconsiderate, uncaring little boy who's never grown up."

"Wow, did you find all those adjectives in the Thesaurus?" joked Chad.

"You're so stupid I'm amazed you know what a Thesaurus is. Let me add one last word--insensitive." With that Laura slammed down the phone.

Chad felt like his whole world was caving in. He wandered down to the kitchen to get a soda. He heard the TV blaring away in the den. His Dad must be getting deaf. He opened the door and saw his Dad fast asleep on the sofa, an empty glass beside him. Chad closed the door gently and walked into the kitchen.

As he pulled open the drawer to find the bottle opener he saw the extra set of his dad's car keys. On impulse he grabbed them and dashed out to the Jag. He could buy his dope and be back before his Dad even knew.

Chad hightailed it out of the driveway. Sarah saw him as she emerged from her studio. She went into the den and was turning the sound down when Hank awoke.

"Hi, Sweetheart. How's the painting going?" Hank sat up and gave her a kiss. "What a day I've had. Last month's profits at the company have plummeted. Then everyone's after me about the stolen money at the club. You'd think I stole it."

"Hank, I'm sorry you've had a bad day. Let me ask you though, did you loan your car to Chad? I saw him leaving the driveway in it."

"You're kidding! I never told that kid he could take the car. I'll kill him when he gets back. I need some aspirin."

The Drummond Home
Monday, June 1st

Laura was fuming when she entered her bedroom. Chad is such a jerk she thought as she pulled her biology book out of her backpack. Forget him and concentrate, she could hear Betsy telling her. Biology was one class she found interesting and had a solid "B" average in it. This helped pull up her "C-" average in math.

Just then Laura's cell phone rang again. When she looked at the caller I.D. the number coming up was unfamiliar. "Hello?"

"Hi, Laura, it's Connie Carson. Your Dad gave me your cell phone number last night. I hope it's not just reserved for friends."

"No, Dr. Carson, my Dad told me he had given you my number. He said you might be talking to me about a mentoring program."

"Yes, Laura, I was part of the same mentoring program myself when I was your age. I was wondering if I might become a mentor to you. By the way, call me Connie."

"Gosh, Dr., er, I mean Connie. I'm really not into school that much. I don't plan on becoming a doctor or lawyer, or anything like that."

"We certainly have athletics in common, Laura. I understand you are an excellent soccer player. They offer wonderful athletic scholarships at my former college. They have a program during the summer after your junior year of high school where you take some pre-college classes and also attend soccer camp. I do know they have some openings left. I would be happy to sponsor you."

Laura was surprised at the confidence Connie seemed to have in her. Was she capable of taking some pre-college classes? Her advisors had always said she could do the work in high school, but that she was lazy. Maybe she could try a little harder. Spending the summer on a college campus might be fun. Maybe Betsy could go, too.

"Connie, I think I would like that very much."

"Good. Maybe I could meet you after school one day this week and we could fill out the papers. The deadline is close. Why don't you discuss it with your Dad, also. Maybe he wouldn't want you away this summer."

"To be honest, I mostly do what I want. Both my Mom and Dad were not home a lot." Laura stopped, thinking maybe she had told Connie too much. It was a relief though to be able to talk to someone about her home life. She had always felt so lonely.

"Some day I'll tell you about my family, Laura. Everyone has family problems. You do need your Dad's permission, however," Connie stated firmly. "Call me when you have it." Laura was getting more excited about the prospect of being on a college campus.

After Laura hung up the phone she went searching for her Dad. She found him in the living room perusing a law journal. "Do you have a minute, Dad?"

"Sure, honey. I'm just trying to review before I start with Chip's firm next week." Peter put his book down and patted the sofa next to him. Laura sat down and blurted out quickly what Connie had presented to her. She mentioned she was worried about leaving him alone so soon after Gloria had just passed away.

"I think it's a wonderful idea, Laura. I'll be busy learning the ropes at my new law office so I might not be home as much as I'd like. This sounds like a great opportunity for you. Go for it." Now that he had given the O.K. Laura put her head on his shoulder.

"Are all boys creeps, Dad?"

"I don't think we can lump all boys in that category, Laura. Are we talking about one specific creep? Could his name be Chad?"

"Oh, Daddy, I feel so used. All Chad cares about is himself. He wasn't even nice when Mom died."

"Laura, sometimes it takes longer for a boy to mature emotionally. I think you're a good judge of character. Cross him off your list. You're so cute the boys will be banging on the front door. By the way, do we need to have any kind of a sex talk?"

Laura squeezed her Dad's arm. "No, Dad, Mom covered that several year's ago. Thanks for making me feel better." Laura stood up to go.

"Laura, if you don't have a lot of homework maybe we could go out for a nice dinner. I was thinking of The Strand. We had a date to do this a few weeks ago. We'll make up for it now."

"Dad, that sounds so nice, but I have a test tomorrow. Could I take a rain check for this weekend?"

"Sure, Laura. I'm glad you're being so diligent about your studies. Maybe we should get you a new dress for our dinner date."

"Great, Dad." Laura hugged Peter and left the room. Peter wondered if he would even be alive after tomorrow to buy the dress. He had no way to pay off the loan shark. Oh, please let them find that money.

The Thunderbird Garage
Monday, June 1st

Jackson, in chauffeur's livery, pulled the limousine up to the garage where Gap Tooth worked. The owner came out of the office. "There's some kind of knocking noise under the car. Can you check it out for me?"

"Sure," replied the owner. "I'll put it on the lift and take a look."

"Wait a minute. I want to get my bag out of the trunk. I've got the evening off, and I don't want to hang with my buddies in these threads."

"Good idea. You can change in the men's room. Go through the office and make a left."

Jackson opened the trunk and lifted out his large duffle bag, careful not to show it was heavy. As the owner called the mechanic, Gap Tooth, to put the limo on the lift, Jackson made his way to the men's room. Chris had told his father that there was an old tool chest stored in the men's room. Vincent thought this would be a good spot to place his surprise for Gap Tooth.

Five minutes later Jackson was standing in the garage looking up at the limo. Now he was wearing a colorful shirt, jeans and boots. The chauffeur's uniform was in the duffle bag which was much lighter.

"You seem to have lost a bracket that holds the exhaust pipe in place. I'm putting a new one on. That should take care of your problem," said Gap Tooth.

Jackson thanked him, fighting for control. He knew this was the guy who got Chris into drugs. When the bill was paid, Jackson tossed his duffle into the trunk and drove away.

At five-fifteen, Jackson pulled the limo up to a pay phone and dialed the local police. Affecting a hip hop speech pattern, Jackson told the desk sergeant that he had bought bad drugs from Gap Tooth at the garage, and the smack made his friends really sick. "Put that Honkey in the slammer," was his closing statement as he hung up.

Police Station
Monday, June 1st

The desk sergeant relayed a call he had received regarding drug sales at the garage to Officers Morrissey and Weeks. As they got into the cruiser, Morrissey grumbled, "What's next? I've spent the day questioning country club types, and men who work for Logrosso Plumbing. No one knows anything about the robbery."

"Logrosso went ballistic when he was told that one of his men was at High Ridge Saturday and Sunday. He claims none of his men worked this past weekend. The country club receptionist who could give us input is on a two week vacation. Now we are sent out to work a drug deal. What's happening to this fine upstanding community?"

Matthew Weeks listened in silence. He was new to the job and to Morrissey's complaints. Weeks wanted to be a good police officer, and he was very careful of what he said and did. He believed in going by the book.

They drove to the garage with no lights flashing and no sirens blaring. Morrissey wanted a quiet look around. Then he planned to go home to a good meal with his wife followed by an evening of television. Maybe he would ask his new partner to join them for dinner.

The Garage
Monday, Five-Thirty p.m., June 1st

Chad, totally infuriated with both Laura and his father, decided he needed some serious drugs to deal with his humiliation. He went to the nearest ATM and cleaned out his account. This money plus the hundred from Sarah's studio gave him a total of three hundred eleven dollars. Here he is, the Captain of the football team and the son of the President of the Country Club, and all he can raise is three hundred and eleven dollars. He felt worthless.

He drove recklessly to the garage. Chad found his father's Jag cornered well at high speeds. If he ever needed a fix, he needed it now. He prayed Gap Tooth would be around. The garage looked quiet as he pulled up. The owner's vintage Thunderbird was not there, but Gap Tooth's pickup was.

Chad parked his father's car beside the garage and hurried inside. Gap Tooth was on the phone when Chad entered the office. "That was great news, Angelo. I'm happy for you in your new job position. I know you won't forget who made your last job come off as smooth as silk." Smiling, Gap Tooth hung up.

"What do you want?" he asked, turning to Chad. "Nice wheels by the way."

"I want a 'big time' score. I need it now."

"Whoa, going for 'big time?' Hope you got the price."

"Don't worry about that. I got it."

"OK," said Gap Tooth. "Sit down and I'll get something that will lift your spirits." He left Chad drumming his fingers on the edge of the office desk and disappeared up the stairs to his living area. Two minutes later he returned with a bag of cocaine.

"This is the same stuff your pal dumped last month. The price is the same, one K. By the way, you can tell your buddy his time to pay is up."

"Forget Chris. I don't have a thousand. Just give me three hundred dollars worth."

Gap Tooth removed a small scale and a plastic bag from the bottom drawer of the desk. He was starting to split the powder when the police cruiser pulled up to the door. The cops could easily see into the office through the glass front.

"Did you bring them here?" Gap Tooth hissed as he frantically tried to get the larger bag out of sight.

Chad went white at the sight of the police. He jumped up, knocked over the scale and spilled powder on the desk and his hand.

Officers Morrissey and Weeks entered the office. Upon seeing the powder Morrissey drew his gun. "Put your hands up and face the wall," barked Morrissey. "Weeks, call for backup."

By seven o'clock six police officers and the chief had combed the premises. They found a stash of drugs in Gap Tooth's room. Most surprisingly, they found one million dollars in the men's room. The money was stuffed into a tool box and strangely, there was play money mixed in with it. The police knew that play money was used to replace the one million dollars stolen the day before from High Ridge Country Club. It was not hard to figure out that this money must be the golf tournament money.

Gap Tooth and Chad were taken to the county jail. The money was sorted, counted and placed in the local bank to be kept in a strong box as evidence.

The LaGrange Home
Monday, Ten p.m., June 1st

Vincent and Chris sat in the den facing each other. The tension in the room was evident in their faces. "Chris, when we sat and talked early last month, I was open with you about my neglect of you and your mother. You were not open with me, however. I trusted you, but you did not trust me. You even went so far as to investigate my family. Why did you behave in that way?" Vincent's eyes were dark and piercing.

Chris looked at his father, took a deep breath and said, "I was stupid. I did not appreciate what you were saying to me. I went from being afraid of you to being afraid of disappointing you. At first I thought I got away with pushing drugs by dumping them during the drug bust. I realized I was wrong when that thug of a drug dealer turned up at our door with the broken sprinkler story."

"Then I was scared to tell you because I didn't tell you earlier. I was a wreck, Dad. I was afraid I'd be hurt by Gap Tooth, and I did not want to lose your good opinion of me. Then as the days went by, and I didn't see Gap Tooth or get any threats, I thought maybe I got away with it. Another stupid idea. Dad, I'm sorry."

Vincent looked at his son very seriously. "Why did you finally tell me?"

"As you know, I looked up our real name, Logrosso. When the police said the robbery was an inside job, and that they were considering Logrosso Plumbing as the crooks, I couldn't hold back. This was my family being framed. Sooner or later they would find out that you were a Logrosso, and your life would never be the same. I had to do something. I told you because I love you." Chris's eyes were filling up, and Vincent saw he was close to breaking up.

"OK," said Vincent. "I admire you coming forth to save the family name. However, I don't like the fact that you were not straight with me. I want you to take a day and come up with a plan as to how you want to be treated for your deception. Meanwhile, I will tell your mother my family history. She is not to hear it from you. Understand?"

"Yes, Dad, but speaking of deception, haven't you practiced all your life what you are accusing me of now?"

"Chris, in a way you are absolutely right. I have paid many times over for having left my immediate family. It was my Mother's idea to get me away from the mob of which my Father was a part. Realize that you have the life you do, because of my Mother's sacrifice and my subsequent lie." Chris nodded and left the room.

The LaGrange House
Tuesday, June 2nd

Valerie was surprised when Vincent told her of his family, but she was also relieved. Now she felt she was living with someone who was real, who had secrets. At the same time, she was not going to share her secret about Peter with Vincent. It was a matter of preserving and keeping Vincent's love for her intact. She truly loved Vincent.

The discussion Vincent and Chris had went well. Chris said he wanted to prove himself to be an adult and trustworthy. He offered to give up his new car. He asked if he could enroll in a college prep program for the summer to be more prepared for his college courses. In his own defense, he stated that he was not slow, just lazy. He wanted to learn how to be a good student. Secretly, he also did not want to feel that Betsy was a better student than he.

Chris also thought that a part time job would teach him how to manage money. He no longer wanted an allowance or credit cards. He wanted his parents to pay for the prep course, but he wanted to support himself other than that.

Now it was Vincent's turn for his eyes to fill up. He cleared his throat and said, "I am very impressed with your ideas, Chris. You show good thinking. I especially like your idea of the prep course."

Police Precinct-
Tuesday, June 2nd

Hank walked up the steps of the police precinct, Chip Nelson by his side. Chad had spent the night in jail due to the fact that a judge couldn't be found to set bail. Chip privately wondered if it wasn't a good thing that Chad saw the inner workings of a prison. Something or someone needs to get through to that kid, he thought. This is one time I can say I'm glad I don't have kids.

It was such a coincidence that the same guy who dealt drugs also stole the million dollars from the club. It wasn't news to be broadcast as yet, but all the money had been recovered.

Chip walked up to the sergeant in charge and explained he was Chad's attorney and would like to talk to him. The sergeant said that Chad was in a holding cell and would be transferred shortly to court for arraignment.

"Sergeant, my client has the right to representation and I want to see him before he goes to court."

"Don't worry, buddy. You can see him now. He was so scared last night he almost shit his pants."

Hank started to go with Chip, but Chip put up his hand. "Better you stay here, Hank. Chad will be more forthright without you there. I need to hear his side of the story." With that Chip was allowed back to see Chad.

Thirty minutes later Chip emerged. "Come on, Hank. Chad is being loaded into a police van and taken to court a block away."

They hurried out the door and arrived at court just as the prisoners were being unloaded.

"Chip, Chad is in handcuffs!" exclaimed Hank.

"This isn't a tea party, Hank. Right now he's a prisoner. I'll explain what happens before we go into the courtroom. You'll sit with the observers and I'll go and sit near the defense attorney's table. Then a court officer named the bridge man calls each case. Chad and I will stand before the judge and plead not guilty. Let's go."

Chip and Hank walk into the courtroom. An hour went by before the bridge man called out "Chad Hawthorne, possession with intent to distribute."

Chad and Chip stood side by side before the judge. The judge said brusquely to Chip, "Plea please."

Chip immediately answered, "Not guilty, your Honor."

The judge, without a trace of emotion, turned to the prosecutor and asked if he had a recommendation for bail.

The prosecutor stated, "Judge, the defendant was arrested with a substantial amount of cocaine in his possession. Since this is a first offense the prosecution requests that bail be set at $25,000."

Chip immediately said, "Your Honor, my client has never been in trouble with the law. He is Captain of the Turner Academy football team, and his parents are prominent citizens in the community."

The judge raised his gavel and said, "ten thousand dollars bail either cash or bond."

Chip and Hank went across the street to the bail bondsman and arranged for Chad's bail. Within half an hour Chad was released to Hank. As they walked down the steps of the courthouse Chad suddenly yelled, "Mom." He flew into his Mother's arms and hugged her tightly.

"Amy Sue, what a surprise," exclaimed Hank. "When I called you yesterday you didn't tell me you were flying here."

"I caught the redeye, Hank. Hello, Chip. I couldn't let my son go through this without support from his Mom." Chad and she were still hugging tightly. Finally she released him and the four started walking.

"Hank, could the three of us have lunch at my hotel? My treat by the way. I think we have things to discuss."

Hank turned to Chip. "I hope you don't mind, Chip. I think it would be good for the three of to talk. Besides, I've not been treated by Amy Sue before."

Chip shook his head. Leave it to Hank to crack a joke during a grave situation. Amy Sue looked as lovely as he remembered her. She actually reminded him a little of Babs.

Speaking of Babs he needed to rush home. She wanted to talk to him about a restaurant she found that was for sale. He thought she'd start with a little "hole-in-the-wall" Italian place, but this sounded upscale and French. He was loaded with money so he'd be happy to make the investment. He looked at Hank and decided those former rumors about Hank and Babs couldn't be true.

"Goodbye, Hank. Nice seeing you, Amy Sue. I'll be meeting with you tomorrow, Chad." Chip walked to his car as the other three caught a cab. They were dropped off at Amy Sue's hotel and went into the dining room.

After ordering lunch, Amy Sue said she had a proposal. "I don't know what the outcome of Chad's trial will be. Whenever everything is straightened out, I thought maybe Chad could come out and live with me. There's a community college nearby and Chad could enroll there. I'm going to marry Jake--he now owns the southern California franchise for all the Fortel Fitness Centers. Chad could work part time at the one close to our house while going to school. What do you say?"

Chad squeezed his Mom's hand. "It sounds great to me, Mom. Pardon me, but I have to pee." Chad got up to go to the men's room.

"Why are we being mommy all of a sudden, Amy Sue? It seems as though you've conveniently forgotten your son for years."

"Hank, I think we've both made mistakes with Chad. All I ever hear from him is that you favor Stephanie and Sarah. I doubt if that is true, but it's how Chad sees things. I thought rather than ping ponging Chad back and forth across the country when he was young, it was better to leave him in a stable household. You were already married to Sarah and I hadn't settled anywhere permanent with Jake."

Hank took Amy Sue's hand. "We'll let Chad decide what he wants to do. I'm certain this drug buying will have some punishment. He's eighteen so will be tried as an adult. Chip seems to think there will be a fine and community service, but no jail time especially if Chad is willing to rat on the dealer. I hope Chip's right."

Chad came back to the table and presented his mother with a rose that he bought in the lobby. "Thanks for coming, Mom. Dad, I'd like to try living with Mom for awhile. Maybe a change of scenery will be good for me."

"OK, Son. Let's try and get your life back on track. I need to get back home. Spend the afternoon with your mother, but be home for dinner. Bye, Amy Sue. See you in another lifetime."

Hawthorne Home--
Tuesday, June 2nd

Hank entered the front door and was greeted by Sarah. "How did it go?"

"Sarah, did you ever think I might've liked your support today?"

"Hank, you know I had an important sitting today--the Barnaby twins are turning four and I'm doing their portrait."

"Maybe Chad's more important. He certainly doesn't feel loved by this family."

"Love is give and take, Hank. I used to try, but I basically gave up when I couldn't reach him. There were so many times he rebuffed me, and kept reminding me I wasn't his mother. I would tell him I didn't expect to take his mother's place, but I think he resented my being your wife."

"I'm sorry, Sarah. I do know you tried. I guess Chad was just striking out at his mother's leaving. You know that bum she left with now owns a bunch of fitness centers."

Hank put his arms around Sarah and held her close. There was no way he could tell her about the despair in his heart. He had decided he wouldn't even attend tonight's meeting at the club. Let them take away his presidency.

About ten o'clock at night the phone rang. It was Jim Lawson. "Hank, I have good news. Since the money has been recovered a majority voted for you to retain your presidency. It was probably wise you stayed away from the meeting tonight. The members felt like you weren't trying to influence them. Of course, I put in a good word, whatever that was worth and so did Connie Carson."

"By the way, Ted Rankin's resignation was accepted tonight. It seems as though any member who took a lesson from him could have a guest play for free. The club sure lost a lot of revenue."

Hank laughed and hung up the phone. He peeked in on Chad and found him sleeping. He remembered when Chad was two. He had an old tattered dog that had to be in his bed at night. Chad would suck his thumb and grasp that dog for dear life.

Amy Sue and he would look at each other like they had created a miracle. They would slip into bed and try to create another little Chad, but no luck. Shortly therafter Amy Sue decided she needed to lose some weight so Hank bought her a membership at a health club. End of story.

He could remember Amy Sue's luscious body. Every curve fitted his hand so well. She seemed leaner now, a little more sleek. Maybe he should go and tell Sarah the good news about his presidency. She might reward him with that soft pliable mouth of hers that made him feel like a man. I wonder if everyone will be surprised when they hear she's pregnant.

Epilogue
Scarsdale December

The front door of the stately Tudor on Elderberry Lane opened to the frosty December morning. Rosie DeAngelo stepped out to retrieve the Westchester Weekly which was lying on the brick walk. She was wearing an elegant LaPerla robe and there were no curlers in her hair which was styled in a fashionable bob.

Rosie took the paper to the table in the atrium which served as a breakfast area. Angelo was eating his eggs over easy with hash browns. The children were in the nearby family room eating their cereal and watching cartoons on the new plasma screen television.

Rosie opened the newspaper to her favorite column, "Close Up with Collette".

"Angelo, the column is extra long this week. You must hear all this gossip." He put down his fork, took her hand and kissed it.

"What's that for?" she asked with a giggle.

"For being you, Rosie, the news announcer. Now read."

"OK, here goes. Mr. and Mrs. Vincent LaGrange have relocated to a sprawling hacienda in the Southwest where their son, Chris, plays freshman football at the University of Arizona.

Dr. Constance Carson and Dr. Edward Williams plan to wed early next spring."

"Mrs. Charles (Babs) Nelson has opened 'La Belle Maison,' a chic French restaurant with an American accent. The cozy ambiance was achieved through the efforts of interior designer Ann Lawson and the art work of Sarah Hawthorne."

"Here's another Lawson in the news. Betsy, Ann and Jim's daughter, has achieved the highest SAT scores ever recorded at Turner Academy. She has been offered a number of scholarships, but seems inclined to pursue her studies in Arizona."

"The money that was evidence in the heist at High Ridge Country Club has finally been released now that the trial is over. The winners of the tournament should be receiving their money within the week."

"It has been announced that Mr. Peter Drummond has joined the law firm of Nelson, Dunn and Peabody. Mr. Drummond's daughter, Laura, has been awarded a soccer scholarship at Boston College."

"So how's that for news, Angelo?"

"Rosie, you're the best." said Angelo as he fixed his expressive blue eyes on her. The speech and image training that Don Vito had recommended for them had paid off. Rosie looked like an upper class lady. She had started to use her middle name, Grace, when mingling with the neighbors. Angelo had to admit to himself that he was happy with the way he looked and spoke, also. They both fit into their new neighborhood very nicely. Yes, he thought, I've done all right.

He smiled as he looked at his comfortable home, his happy kids and his innocent and lovable wife.

My Grandmother would be proud of her boy. My Grandmother, Anna Marie Logrosso.

Aftermath of the Heist

The actual money taken at the heist was never found, much to Vincent LaGrange's relief. Gap Tooth practiced Omerta and never revealed details of the heist. He accepted his punishment of five years in prison for which he was greatly rewarded.

About the Author

Margaret Flynn, a Brooklyn native of Bath Beach has published research on the language of Brooklyn (Brooklynese). She provides an up close insight into the everyday life of organized crime.

Margaret has appeared on national television and radio networks, and on the BBC discussing Brooklyn and its language. Her interviews with the Associated Press have appeared nationwide and in Europe.

Arlene Scollar, co-author, started golf at the age of seven. She won her first club championship at the age of nineteen at Grosse Ile, Michigan. Arlene was on the first women's golf team at the University of Michigan. After graduating with a degree in Journalism, she taught in the public school system.

Arlene has been Staten Island, New York Amateur Champion three times as well as club champion at several Staten Island courses.

Book Club Questions

1. In regard to an image of ourselves:

"We are as we see ourselves
We are as others see us
We are as we think others see us."

How is this concept prevalent throughout the novel?

2. We all recognize that we are influenced by society. How are the characters in this novel influenced by the society where they live?

3. What did the Mafia members think of the country club society?

4. We often hear people say he/she is just like his/her parent. Do you believe this is an accurate statement?

What characters in this book resemble their parents in appearance and/or action?

5. We have all experienced advice and direction from our parents and people who are parent figures.

When do we find this kind of relationship taking place in the book?

6. One of the characters goes off to have plastic surgery in a foreign country. How do you weigh doing things for your betterment while not neglecting your family?

Is this sending a message that we shouldn't be content with our bodies? True or false?

7. Is it possible to escape your past?

Who in the book tries to do this? Was he/she successful? Why?

8. Were there any characters that you disliked? Liked? Were there any characters that you would like to see their role expanded?

9. One of the characters is punished for having an illegal substance but another is not. Did this offend you?

10. Did it bother you that Peter played in the golf tournament after his wife had just passed away?

11. We all come from a family. There are two kinds of families in this book: blood relatives and the Mafia.

How are these two types of families similar? How are they different?

12. All of the characters had stressful moments. How did Vincent, Chris and Gloria battle their own stress?

13. What did you like the best about the book? What did you like the least?

Would you recommend it to a friend?

Printed in the United States
135398LV00001B/5/P